SISTER CARMEN

M. CORVUS

Translated from the German by KATE DYKERS

1st WORLD
LIBRARY
Literary Society

Sister Carmen

M. Corvus

© 1st World Library – Literary Society, 2004
PO Box 2211
Fairfield, IA 52556
www.1stworldlibrary.org
First Edition

LCCN: 2005901356

Softcover ISBN: 1-4218-1171-5
Hardcover ISBN: 1-4218-1071-9
eBook ISBN: 1-4218-1271-1

Purchase *"Sister Carmen"*
as a traditional bound book at:
www.1stWorldLibrary.org/purchase.asp?ISBN=1-4218-1171-5

1st World Library Literary Society is a nonprofit
organization dedicated to promoting literacy by:

- Creating a free internet library accessible from any
  computer worldwide.
- Hosting writing competitions and offering book
  publishing scholarships.

Sister Carmen
contributed by Tim, Ed & Rodney
in support of
1st World Library Literary Society

CHAPTER I.

The first rays of early dawn threw their shadowy light over hill and dale, and all nature seemed animated with new life as the fresh spring breeze kissed the young blades of grain in the fields. Ever brighter and more glowing grew the eastern horizon, ever more golden the light, floating clouds, until at last the dazzling rays of the king of day flashed forth upon the expectant world.

With its clear carol of joy, a lark soared upward from her dewy nest, singing her morning anthem to the great Creator; and, as if in glad sympathy with the happy bird, the many and varied voices of nature united in celebrating the resurrection, not only of the sun, but of all things, for it was Easter Sunday morning.

Forth from the dwellings of a small Moravian village issued a band of simply attired folk, who wended their way through the green fields and up the hillside to a spacious wood, where was located a quiet graveyard, in which gigantic linden-trees stretched out their leafless branches, forming a graceful network overhead.

In the centre of this lovely spot stood an immense stone cross, the sign of that Lord whose resurrection was to-day celebrated with the sound of trumpets and the voices of the people.

A feeling of holy joy seemed to reign in every heart, as the crowd stood grouped around the base of the cross, gazing with reverence at it as it now shone bathed in the glorious radiance of the risen sun. Presently the music ceased and the soft echoes died away among the distant hills, while a clear, manly voice in the midst of the congregation proclaimed: "The Lord is risen!" "He is risen indeed!" replied each one joyously; after which the first speaker advanced nearer to the cross and addressed a few words to the people:

"My dear brothers and sisters, in accordance with our usual custom, we visit to-day our beautiful cemetery, not to mourn for our dead, but to rejoice that our Lord has risen from the grave to give us eternal life; for with Him shall rise all those who follow in His holy footsteps here below. Therefore, as we put not on the garb of mourning, let us not grieve in our hearts when we think of our loved ones who have gone home before us, but clasp each other's hands and be glad together, that through the blessed Redeemer such happiness has been vouchsafed to them. For His sake, and for the preservation of the true faith, the Moravians wandered forth from their fatherland, forsaking the wealth and luxuries of this world; but they took with them that which was more precious than all else, the pure, unadulterated truths of the Gospel, and sought a new country, in which they might dwell, and preserve their religion forever. In the wilds of a strange land they found a resting-place; and in the community were retained the old statutes and laws, the old forms of worship, the old brotherly love and kindness, which from the earliest period had characterized them. From this little seed-corn which was then planted, the Moravians have spread out their branches into all parts of the world. Let us remain faithful to the principles which united our forefathers; let us ever hold sacred the religion for the sake of which they suffered, and to which they firmly adhered, in spite of persecution and peril. Hold fast brotherly love! Forgive and bear with one another in love, sacrifice yourselves for love's sake, suffer and die, in charity with all men, - then are you true disciples of the Lord. Amen!"

The preacher's voice ceased, and the congregation devoutly

echoed his "Amen." After a short pause the assembly broke up, with hearty hand-shakings and joyful greetings. In little groups of twos and threes they rambled through the beautiful grounds where the loved ones were laid to rest. The members of the fraternity, as they conversed in low but cheerful tones, bore a close resemblance to one another in the quiet simplicity of their attire. There was no pretension to ornament or style; cleanliness seemed the only adornment sought for, and it certainly did reign supreme. The women and girls wore small, close-fitting white caps, the different-colored ribbons on them distinguishing the various classes, and giving a very pleasing effect to the scene. The wives were recognized by blue ribbons on their caps, and the widows by white, while the older girls wore pink and the younger ones bright red. Gradually all returned to their homes in the valley below, where lay the thriving Moravian village.

One young girl, however, remained behind alone, lost in thought and quite unconscious that her companions had already taken their way homeward. Leaning against one of the large linden-trees, whose ancient trunk completely screened her slim figure, she stood, looking downward on the beautiful landscape which lay before her admiring eyes. Mountain and valley, forest and field, were bathed in the golden sunshine. Nothing was yet in bloom, but in every swelling bud there seemed to lie a foreshadowing of coming glory.

"Sister Carmen, hast thou not noticed that thy companions have returned with their elders, and that thou art left alone?" suddenly asked a deep masculine voice at her side.

She involuntarily shrank back, as if from fear - was it because she was alone, or was she only startled from her dreaming? - and looked timidly at the speaker. He was a man well advanced in years; his hair partially gray, but his complexion retaining much of its youthful freshness and color; and there was some difficulty in determining his age.

Although his brow was thoughtful and his grave eyes habitually looked upward with an expression of calm serenity and humble piety, yet the curve of his mouth, around which there lurked a peculiar smile, contradicted the idea of sanctity.

"Have they really left me, Brother Jonathan? I had entirely forgotten how time was passing, in the tumult of joyful feelings which filled my heart," said the girl with a sunny smile.

"It gladdens my heart, dear sister, to know it gives you such great joy to celebrate the Resurrection of our Lord," he replied. "Truly it is a blessed privilege to be able to lose one's self in the contemplation of holy things, and, forgetting the cares of this present life, rejoice in the hope of heaven, and be as one dead to every temporal joy."

"But I was not thinking at all of the life beyond the grave, only of this present one. How beautiful it is, and what happiness to be able to enjoy it!" she said candidly, as her youthful countenance lighted up with a glowing expression of love of life and pleasure.

Hers was a singularly beautiful face, on which the man at her side gazed with open admiration. The close-fitting cap, with its bright red bow, indicated that the girl had not yet reached her eighteenth year. Here and there peeped out little truant locks of the glossy black hair, whose richness and abundance the close covering could not entirely conceal or fetter. The broad, intellectual brow; the delicate, pencilled lashes, from the shadow of which shone forth lustrous black eyes that flashed with intelligence and spirit; the arched nose, with its slightly dilated nostrils; pouting mouth, with full, cherry lips, all gave her something of a proud expression, which was, however, softened by the beaming smile which so often lighted it up. Although only a faint color tinged her cheek, yet the clear, brunette complexion glowed with fresh, warm, young life, and the slender, lithe form that leaned with such childlike abandon against the old tree displayed the most exquisite symmetry.

"Yes, this present life is certainly very pleasant, dear sister," he resumed, approaching yet nearer to her; and he indeed seemed to find it so as he contemplated this fair, blooming, delightful young creature. "We do wisely to enjoy it, and use it as a means to prepare us for the great hereafter, accomplishing that end all the more effectually when we love the Lord, and, through Him, one another. Sister Carmen, did you listen to the beautiful discourse on brotherly and sisterly love which our honored presbyter gave us to-day?" and the speaker bent his head so low that she felt his hot breath on her cheek, and his heavy hand on her shoulder. But quickly turning aside and withdrawing from his touch, she replied: "Yes, I heard it, and it is indeed a very good and proper thing to love one another; but I think it is not always love which is called so, or seems so;" and her mouth twitched with a repressed smile, as if some secret thought amused her.

"Dear sister, how can you speak thus?" he said. "Men, it is true, are weak, and often swerve from their duty; but we should help each other in the spirit of love, so that we may be all united and grow to resemble each other in character."

"Resemble each other in character!" She repeated his words musingly, and the gaze from her dark eyes wandered away off, beyond her companion. "Can we ever do that? God has created us so different; if He had wished us all to be alike, would He not have made us so?"

The man looked at her earnestly, and an expression of disapproval passed over his face as he answered: "Any one, to hear you speak in that way, and not know you as well as I do, would never believe that you had lived so long among us and were one of us. I have known you always, ever since you were a wee, toddling thing. It was in Jamaica, when I went to your father from the mission."

Carmen blushed deeply at the rebuke which lay in his words, and, as if to atone, said quickly:

"Oh, forgive me! I am sure I would gladly be like you all if I only could. But I cannot always be calm and serene, as every one else here is; and I fear our dear Sister Agatha, with all her endeavors, will succeed as little in changing me, as you do in trying to produce the same degree of health in every one, even though you be the wise and learned Doctor Jonathan Fricke. Each bird sings after its own fashion, and although all are different, yet none are bad. I cannot believe every one is culpable who does not pass through life calmly and sedately, as we endeavor to do. It surely cannot be wrong for people to laugh, and dance! Dance!" and she laughed outright, so that her pearly teeth gleamed from between the rosy lips. "It must be enchanting to skip round and round to the sound of merry music!" She had allowed herself to be carried away by enthusiasm, and spoke louder than was consistent with Moravian decorum, or suitable to the place where she was. Her eyes sparkled, and the dainty little foot which peeped forth from under her dress seemed altogether suited to trip with fairy fleetness through the merry mazes of the dance.

One glance, however, at her companion recalled her to the present. Her eyes sank, the little foot was hastily withdrawn, and she wrapped more closely about her the dark shawl which had slipped from her shoulders.

"But the time! the time!" she stammered. "It is getting later and later while we are chatting, and Sister Agatha will have good cause to be vexed with me."

With fleet steps she hurried through the quiet graveyard, down the hill, and along the path which led to the dwellings of the settlement. Jonathan stood looking after her, as long as his eye could discern the airy, lithe figure.

All pretence of calmness had vanished from his face. His

eyes glittered with a strange light and glowed with passionate desire. For a moment the staid, elderly man was transformed into an eager, ardent youth.

"She inherits the hot, proud Spanish blood of her mother, and, alas! the same fatal, enchanting beauty also," he muttered. "If I could only win her -" He stopped abruptly, as if fearful of being overheard, and began to brush away some imaginary specks of dust from his sleeve. Drooping his head into its usual pious attitude, his face assumed its former grave expression, and he was again the sedate, quiet Brother.

CHAPTER II.

A Moravian settlement! As we enter it, it seems as if we stepped into another sphere, so utterly unlike is it to the bustle and hurry of the age of progress which prevails in the outer world that presses so closely upon its borders, and against which it quietly but firmly opposes the bulwarks of its ancient customs, the simplicity of its regulations, and the severity of its discipline. It has no intercourse with the tide of human life surging around it. It seems like a small body of Christians, left from the Apostolic age, that after being buried for centuries has been dug out in later days. The government of the community resembles that of a large family bound together by ties of love; all its members are brothers and sisters, divided, according to age, sex, and conditions of life, into bands called choruses, at the head of each an elder, either male or female, presiding and superintending its spiritual affairs and enforcing its daily discipline. Each elder gives in a report of all that occurs in the chorus to the Conference, as this is the chief board of management in the society. There is, therefore, nothing which transpires in the life of any individual that is not brought before this tribunal.

About ten o'clock one morning, an elegant carriage, drawn by two spirited horses, passed through the quiet, scrupulously clean streets of the settlement, and drew up at the door of the hotel, or, as they call it, the general lodging-house; and from the vehicle sprang a young and very distinguished-looking gentleman with erect, military bearing and noble features. He was followed by a lady, and a young girl of about twelve years of age, and a tall, lanky lad who had not yet lost his boyish awkwardness.

"Unharness and take the trunk to the Sisters' house," said the gentleman to the coachman.

The newly-arrived guests entered the sitting-room, which was entirely unoccupied, and whose clean, freshly-sanded floor seemed almost to shine with a consciousness of its own spotlessness. The host, a quiet old man, entered to receive their commands, which he attended to in person. Everything was done silently; not even the plates and glasses rattled as they were placed on the-table; and when all was prepared, the man left the room, not attempting, after the manner of hosts in general, to enter into conversation with his guests, or to ply them with questions as to whence they came, whither they were going, etc.

The lady, a very remarkable-looking woman, was apparently the mother of the three others, but seemed young to be the parent of the eldest, who had evidently numbered thirty years.

The breakfast, which was excellent and well served, was quickly disposed of; and dinner being ordered for two o'clock, the little party left the house. On the street, the same stillness, the same absence of people prevailed as elsewhere.

"Do you know the way to the Sisters' house, mother?" asked the young man of the lady as they led the way, the two younger ones following behind.

"Of course, Alexander," she replied. "I was here once, some years ago, on a visit to President von Karsdorf, and I can perfectly remember how full of interest the whole place was, and how pleased the Karsdorfs were to think they could end their lives in this peaceful, quiet spot."

"Such extraordinary order and cleanliness seems almost like

a matter of pride and show on the part of these humble people - as if the inner purity of their souls must needs be manifested in this extreme, outward neatness," said the gentleman, laughing.

"You are prejudiced against the Moravian character, I know, and yet there is so much that is good in them!" argued the lady.

"That may well be so, mother. I am willing to acknowledge all their good qualities," said her son; "but these numerous forms which intrude themselves upon every occasion seem like fetters and bonds to free souls. So much unnatural restraint and parade of sanctity is offensive to me. I never could tolerate hypocrites, and such they surely must be, although, of course, they would be shocked at the idea; for under all this excessive humility, this parade of piety, I venture to say there lies much concealed of which we do not dream. One can imagine how much Herr von Karsdorf, an old epicure and man of the world, must have dissimulated to conform himself to the manners of this community, to be allowed to end his days here."

His mother shook her head. "I think," she said, "that the subdued, pious bearing of the members has become like a second nature to them, and is now, therefore, not hypocritical. Besides, think how excellent is the domestic economy of the settlement; how active and prosperous they are in trade and various industries. They have many practical, temporal, as well as spiritual objects to which they devote themselves."

"I grant all that; but such immense importance is attached to little things. Their work would be very trifling and ridiculous if attempted on a large scale. It resembles the wonderful industry in an ant-hill, unremitting and earnest, but petty labor. No genius is displayed. What great men have arisen from among them? Who are the distinguished scholars and artists which have gone forth from their ranks?"

"And how about their sufferings?" interposed the other, quickly. "Their struggles amidst privation and misery, and persecutions of all kinds in distant lands, for the sake of their faith, and to rescue wild heathens from depravity and barbarism, and win them over to the Christian religion? Do you not deem that a noble work? Consider their admirable regulations as regards education; are they not excellent? I look for the greatest improvement in Adele, as the result of her stay here. - But it seems to me I have turned into the wrong street, for the Sisters' house is certainly not here!"

"Here come some people at last," replied Alexander - "a girl with a child. They will be able to direct us." He stepped forward to meet the approaching figures, and with a polite greeting begged for information. The young girl dropped a modest courtesy to the stranger, and with downcast eyes listened to his inquiries about the way to the Sisters' house. Then she turned to the lady, who had in the mean time drawn near, and said courteously: "I am just going hither; may I conduct you?"

"You would oblige us exceedingly," replied the lady, kindly.

"What a lovely Sister! It wouldn't be such a bad thing to be a Brother here," whispered Alexander to his mother. He did not speak too low for the sensitive ear of the girl to catch his words, for she blushed deeply, and the rosy little mouth curled proudly and defiantly. Visibly offended, she turned away from the gentleman, and simply saying "Come" to the lady, walked on ahead, leading the little child by the hand, and giving no apparent heed to the party behind.

Retracing their steps for a short distance, they turned into a side street, and here - wonder of wonders! - were some more people. A horse stood, saddled and bridled, before the door of one of the houses, and a man was just in the act of mounting. He did not seem to be a particularly expert horseman, or his steed the most patient of animals; for the former displayed his awkwardness in attempting to mount, and the latter, as soon as he became aware of his master's intention, kicked, and sprang aside. The man sought to quiet him, patted his neck, and once more tried the difficult task of getting on his back; but the sight of the approaching strangers now added to his clumsiness, and rendered him even more helpless than before. He had scarcely put his foot in the stirrup, when the animal pranced, kicked and reared, jerking the reins from his owner's hands, and throwing him down on the pavement; after which he started at full speed down the street, directly towards the advancing party. As soon as the horse showed a disposition to be restive, the girl had led the child close up against the side of the house, and looking back at the strangers following her, she observed an expression of contempt on the young man's face, as he watched the awkward movements of the Brother; being himself a skilful rider and able, with his supple yet powerful frame, to master even the wildest horse.

When the man fell to the ground, and the unrestrained animal came rapidly onward, the strangers also moved hastily aside. But the little child had, in its fright, broken loose from the girl's hand, and ran into the middle of the street to pick up a ball which had rolled from its hand. A cry of horror broke from every lip, and in another moment the child would have been dashed under the horse's hoofs as she stooped to pick up the toy. But before the girl could reach the little one, the strange gentleman, with one long stride, was on the spot, and had seized the child in his arms. With a firm hand he grasped the reins, and brought the terrified beast to a standstill by sheer strength. It all happened so quickly that, looking at the child playing merrily with its ball a moment after, one could almost have fancied it was all a dream. The girl, who had turned as pale as death, was leaning against the side of the house; but quickly regaining her self-control, she hastened to her little charge, saying, with trembling voice, as she shyly glanced at its preserver, "I thank you, sir; you have saved the little one entrusted to me from great peril."

The unfortunate rider who had been thrown now came limping up, and was profuse with his thanks to this "friend in need."

There was such a very remarkable contrast between the two men, as they now stood side by side, that it struck the eye of every one present, even the young girl's. The humble bearing and uncouth figure of the Brother looked decidedly unprepossessing compared with the tall, elegant form of Alexander, which, with all its agility and grace, was full of power, as if forged from steel. Every muscle was still strained by the exertion just made; his face was flushed, his blue eyes sparkled with the fire of inward strength of will, and yet the expression showed no evidence of agitation, only quiet consciousness of power. While he yet held the reins with his left hand, he assisted the other man, who finally succeeded in gaining the saddle.

"A vicious animal, sir," said Alexander to the other, handing him the bridle. "He seems to be skittish, and will not admit of any joking; spare the spur, and keep firm hold on the bridle until you are sure of yourself."

Thus saying, he stood aside, and man and horse proceeded on their way.

"And, now, if you will be so good, miss, please continue to be our guide," he said, turning toward the girl.

They soon reached the Sisters' house. "Ah, yes, this is the very place!" cried the lady, joyfully. "Thank you most sincerely for your courtesy, dear child. Will you kindly tell us which door to enter? We gave notice by letter of our coming, and are expected. I am Frau von Trautenau; these are my two sons, and this is my little daughter, whom I am bringing to stay here." She offered her hand cordially to the girl, and looked kindly at her beautiful face.

"I beg that you wilt enter this way, into the parlor," was the modest reply, as the maiden opened a door on the first floor. "I will inform Sister Agatha of your arrival."

It was not long ere the gentle Sister made her appearance. She was a friendly, motherly-looking woman, on whose gray hair was placed a cap with a pink bow, the badge of the unmarried Sisters. She greeted the visitors with dignified cordiality.

"Forgive me for bringing my entire family, and allow me to present each member to you," said Frau von Trautenau, after the first words of welcome.

"My stepson Alexander, captain of infantry, and my trusty adviser and support since my husband's death; my son Hans, and my daughter Adele, your pupil from this time forward, whom I commend most earnestly to your kindness and care."

Sister Agatha took the child most affectionately in her arms, and pressing a kiss on her brow, said sweetly:

"You must confide in me, dear child, as if I were your mother, and I will consider you a sacred trust committed to me. We are all a large family of Sisters here, who love one another, learning cheerfully and working diligently. 'Pray and work!' This golden proverb is our motto through the day, and the love and industry which you will see everywhere will soon teach you to feel at home among us."

"I live, as you know, in the neighborhood," said Frau von Trautenau, as Adele looked up tearfully. "Our estate, Wollmershain Grove, is only a few hours' ride from here, and sometimes, if I drive in, you will, I suppose, allow Adele to visit us for a little recreation?"

"Oh, certainly, Frau Von Trautenau," returned Sister Agatha - "in vacation. May I now show you our apartments and arrangements, so that you may know exactly how your dear little girl will be situated?"

"I shall be delighted," replied the lady. "Everything here interests us, of course, in the highest degree."

With that, they all rose and followed the sister.

CHAPTER III.

"We require a great deal of room," explained Sister Agatha, as they passed along, "as there are separate apartments, not only for the pupils, but also for the unmarried Sisters of our community, who are not members of a family and yet live and work here with us. Indeed, even those who have families in the outside world often come to us to employ their unoccupied time." So saying, she led her guests from the first floor to the second, and from one room to another. Everything was neatly and simply arranged. The modest dress of the Sisters, with their little white caps, their calm diligence in spite of the exhilarating air of this bright morning, their quiet gait and subdued voices, the deep silence which pervaded the house, gave one the sensation of being in a cloister. Sister Agatha conducted the party into the general workroom. It was built like a deep hall. At long tables sat numbers of girls with every variety of countenance; all young, not quite grown, gathered in separate groups, busy with needlework or writing. The elder ones seemed to supervise the younger and instruct them in their work. Amongst these was the girl who had acted the part of guide to the strangers. All rose at the entrance of the visitors, and after a moment silently resumed their seats.

"Here you see the children of our members, and our dear pupils, all together. They are sent to us from the most remote colonies and missions to be educated, and they very soon learn to consider themselves one with us. Dear Sister Marie," said Agatha, turning to one of the girls, "please tell Frau Von Trautenau where you were born." The child addressed, a little girl with olive complexion and keen black eyes, arose, like a piece of machinery, on being spoken to, and replied: "At Paramaribo, in Surinam," and dropped back into her seat.

"And you, dear Sister Genevieve?"

"At St. Jean, in the West Indies."

"And Sister Sarah?" "At Sarepta, in Russia, in the province of Saratow."

"Sister Jacobi?"

"At Batavia, in Java."

"Sister Carmen?"

Similarly to all those called before, Carmen rose also, when Sister Agatha mentioned her name; but it seemed an involuntary motion, as if in obedience to a command, and then, after a second's hesitation, she at once resumed her seat. During the entire proceedings her glance had wandered with painful eagerness, now to Frau von Trautenau, now to her eldest son, and had remarked how this questioning of the girls had seemed to amuse them. At last, when her name was called, a deep blush suffused Carmen's lovely face, and she could not summon courage to answer.

"Dear Sister Carmen!" repeated the Superior, as if she thought Carmen had not heard the first call.

"Oh, please -" now interposed Frau von Trautenau, endeavoring to assist the girl when she saw her painful confusion. She stroked back from Carmen's brow the curly locks which had escaped from under the edge of the little white cap, saying: "Never mind! I can fancy, from her pretty name, that her cradle was rocked in Spain, if not in a still more distant and beautiful clime. Is it not so, dear child?"

There was so much delicate consideration in the tone and manner of Frau von Trautenau towards the embarrassed girl that Carmen, with an impulse of sincere gratitude, bent over her friendly hand and kissed it.

"Yes, it is so," She said, looking at the lady, with her dark eyes full of childlike innocence. "I was born in the beautiful West Indies, on the island of Jamaica."

"Have you been here long?"

"Oh yes, a very, very long time. I was sent here when only nine years old, to be educated, my mother having died some time before; and my father left Jamaica a year after I did, to go to the East Indies. I have not seen him or heard from him once since then."

Carmen said all this in an undertone, and her voice trembled, as if full of suppressed tears.

"Poor child! how sorry I am for you!" said the lady, affectionately, taking Carmen's hand and pressing it tenderly. She felt such a deep sympathy for the lonely girl that she quickly added: "Since you know so well what it is to be separated from loved ones, will you not try to interest yourself a little in Adele? She will perhaps find it difficult at first to reconcile herself to this new life."

"Gladly, with all my heart, if your daughter will confide in me!" replied Carmen with joy.

A stroke of the clock, which sounded loudly through the quiet house, announced the hour of the midday meal. The girls rose at once from their places, and Frau von Trautenau took leave of Sister Agatha, taking her daughter with her.

After the departure of the guests, the girls left the room;

and as Carmen passed Sister Agatha, the latter laid her hand on the girl's shoulder, saying gravely, but not unkindly:

"Dear Sister, I would like to speak with you; on your return from the love-feast which we celebrate this evening, come to my room, and I will have a talk with you."

Carmen looked calmly into the serious eyes of the speaker, where she read no small degree of secret dissatisfaction.

"Yes, Sister Agatha, I will come."

* * * * * *

No apartment could be more simply furnished than that of Sister Agatha. It seemed as if she wished to excel in her avoidance of anything like unnecessary ornament or comfort. Three chairs, a table, an old-fashioned sofa, a writing-desk, and a chest of drawers formed the scanty furniture. The walls were whitewashed and bare, while at the windows were hung plain white curtains. Above the desk was placed the solitary ornament of the room, the watchword for the day. These "watchwords" are texts of Scripture printed on cards, one for each day in the year, and distributed to every member of the settlement, so that all may meditate upon it, and guide their daily lives by its precepts.

Sister Agatha sat at one of the windows; and with her, his chair drawn back into the shadow, out of the bright afternoon sunshine, sat Brother Jonathan Fricke, talking in his calmest and most deliberate manner, "It seems to me, dear Sister, that the healthy give you more anxiety than the sick."

"Because they are the more difficult to help than others; and although your visit is principally to the sick, I should like to have your advice regarding the case of one in my charge, and whose father was your dearest friend."

"You are anxious about Carmen's worldly-mindedness; but ought you not to be indulgent, dear Sister, and remember that the child's early associations are still holding sway in her heart, and make great excuse for her? Brother Mauer, you remember, went away from the mission to his plantation, where, although he did not sever himself from our communion, there was not much to remind him of his religious obligations. His last wife, a hot-blooded Creole, could not be considered much help as regards keeping the faith. She loved best to swing herself into the saddle and gallop away over the plains. She would sing her glowing Spanish songs to the accompaniment of the mandolin; or else she would dance like a fairy, her foot scarce seeming to touch the floor as she floated along, to the sound of the tambourine played by her old negro duenna. She was too beautiful for him to restrain, in dancing, riding, or anything. Too beautiful!" he repeated, becoming more and more enthusiastic. "I have seen her often, when summoned to the plantation on professional duty as a physician; and there was little Carmen, always with her mother, and following her in everything. She learned to dance and sing in true Spanish style, and she seemed to feel all the beauty and fascination of it."

Suddenly he paused, as if becoming conscious of his unwonted animation under the wondering gaze of Sister Agatha's grave eyes. Heaving a deep sigh, he had again recourse to his old trick of brushing an invisible speck of dust from his sleeve, and then continued in the orthodox, placid manner:

"It was a fearful sin for a member of our faith to fall into, and Brother Mauer should have resisted the temptation. I spoke to him frequently about it, but he had lost all power of self-control. He was too much absorbed in love for his wife, and therefore it was a mercy to his soul and Carmen's that this Spanish girl died, and the child was placed here, under our discipline, where she may yet be won over to a spiritual life," he concluded, and cast a humble, sanctimonious look on Sister Agatha.

"Where were you when her mother died?" asked the Sister. "Were you with her?"

"No; she has been dead about ten years, and I left Jamaica some time before that, as my health could not stand the climate. I went from there to the northern part of the United States. From Bethlehem, where I remained several years, I went back to the old place, and when I got there Carmen was a wee little maiden, and I was told that Brother Mauer had left Jamaica for the East Indies."

"Well, surely the Lord called him to be His instrument," interrupted Sister Agatha. "It was wonderful how he was seized with such an irrepressible desire to be a missionary. And as far as we can know, he has worked without flagging for the faith. All news from him has ceased for some time now; and is it not strange that he has never made any application for money? He took only a very small sum with him when he went on his mission, and the large sum which the sale of his lands in Jamaica brought is still in a bank in this country."

"Has he, then, left nothing for Carmen?"

"We receive a certain interest from the money, for her support and education," replied Agatha, "but it is, comparatively speaking, very little. The money must have accumulated to an immense sum by this time. If her father is dead, Carmen must be a very wealthy heiress - another temptation for her, poor child! It is strange we hear nothing from Brother Mauer. I feel sure he must be dead - died while working for his Lord!"

As she spoke, Jonathan's eyes flashed, and he suddenly lifted his head; but remembering where he was, he immediately resumed his usual pious bearing, and, when Agatha ceased speaking, said, with something like a sigh:

"He was my friend!"

A pause ensued, during which he seemed lost in reflection.

"It does seem as if we have lost him," he continued, "and Carmen must be an orphan. Poor child! Bear so much the more leniently with her, dear Sister; and if from time to time you observe signs of her early training, and that her impulses carry her sometimes beyond what is quite becoming, remember she will find in me a guide who is ever ready to lead her in the right way."

"Truly, you are still the same faithful friend to her father, for you have so much consideration for his child," said Agatha, deeply affected. "But believe me, dear Brother, I also love the girl with my whole heart, and am the more anxious for that reason, lest her natural inclinations may lead her into error. But to whom shall I direct her for guidance, if not to the dear Lord Himself?"

"Surely, my Sister, you say well; and therefore it would be better for her to have a helpmate ever at her side, who would remind her of her holy calling," returned Jonathan, earnestly. "Next week she will be eighteen years of age, and will then be numbered among the marriageable sisters. It would certainly be the best thing for her to have a husband; therefore seek one for her, Sister Agatha; and if you and the assembly of elders can find no one better, then will I, for the sake of her welfare, give up the freedom of my single life and take her to myself, to be to her a faithful protector and husband, for the glory of God."

While speaking, he had risen nervously from his seat, and leaning one arm on the back of the chair, uttered the last words hastily, as if impelled thereto by a sudden over-whelming emotion. His eyes were fixed on the floor, only once in a while looking furtively up, as if to watch the effect of his words. But the Sister's open countenance showed only a joyful surprise.

"You would really sacrifice yourself for Sister Carmen's benefit?" she cried. "How can I do otherwise than approve, dear Brother? You, the pious, wise, experienced physician, full of love and kind forbearance towards her, and knowing so well, all the while, what is for her good! Where in all the wide world could she ever find a better counsellor and guide?"

"Nay, say not so, Sister Agatha," he interrupted reprovingly. "No sinful creature deserves such praise; least of all I. None of us are more than humble instruments for good, and have no merit at all of ourselves."

"Yet, my dear Brother, we cannot but recognize the good in others," replied she in a gentle tone. "And I say no more than the truth. If every one as worthy as you had only a portion of your modesty! The sick long for you and praise you as their benefactor; the well welcome you everywhere as a friend and adviser. Let me thank you for offering yourself to Carmen, for you have done so with true kindness and love. After the feast this evening, I will communicate your proposal to the elders; and if they consent to it, then, afterwards, I will speak to Carmen on the subject. I have notified her to come to me, without reference to this matter, as I want to make some inquiries about her behavior this morning. But now it is the hour for evening prayer."

She arose, and extended her hand to Jonathan, who returned its hearty pressure. Never had his manner been more humble than it now was as he left the room. But when the door was closed behind him, he stood quite still for a moment, and the disagreeable expression of his mouth was greatly enhanced by the smile of triumph which lit up his countenance.

"Ah!" he exclaimed under his breath, "beauty and wealth; they will indeed compensate for the past."

CHAPTER IV.

When Frau von Trautenau, with her family, entered the spacious prayer-room, to be present at the love-feast, the mass of the congregation had already assembled, and were singing to the accompaniment of the organ. The lady accepted the places assigned to her and Adele by Sister Agatha, but Alexander and his brother took possession of an empty bench near the door.

The room presented a strange appearance for a place of worship. It was destitute of any ornament whatever. The altar, which was at one end, consisted of a simple wooden table, on which stood a large crucifix. The brothers and sisters sat at long tables covered with white linen; but, as usual, the sexes were seated apart. Each member was served with a small cup of tea and a little bun.

After a while the music ceased, and a long prayer by the principal elder followed after which another member read a letter from one of their missionaries, Joseph Hubner, who was at work in the land of the Kaffres. This letter presented a touching picture of humble self-sacrifice and sincere devotion.

Alexander felt deeply moved, and forgot the strange mixture of religious exercises and temporal enjoyment which this feast displayed. Absorbed in listening, he did not observe that, in his immediate vicinity, a singular commotion had arisen, and that a good deal of whispering was carried on among the Brothers, as they regarded him and Hans with curious glances. After the reading of the letter another hymn was given out; then Hans nudged his brother.

"What is there so peculiar about us? Everybody is gazing at us so!"

Alexander glanced about, to see if anything was wrong, but could discover nothing amiss. They had quietly and politely partaken of the feast when it was offered to them, yet something must be wrong to create such a sensation; so he turned to some one sitting near by, with the question:

"Are we depriving any one of this seat?"

"Oh no, indeed, my dear sir," he replied.

"So much the better," said Alexander. "We do not wish to cause any inconvenience and I began to fear we were doing so."

"I must ask your pardon," stammered the Brother, with much confusion. "It was certainly very rude for us to stare at you so, and yet it was the result of the deep sympathy we feel for your brother, who seems so young to be a widower."

Alexander gave a searching glance at the speaker, to see if he was ridiculing his brother. Hans a widower! In spite of his tall stature, he showed very plainly that he was but an overgrown schoolboy.

"A widower, sir!" said the young man, slowly. "My brother is only sixteen years old, and is still at school. In the world we do not marry at that age."

"It did indeed seem very strange to me," said the good man, in extreme embarrassment; "but being seated among the widowers, we judged it must be so."

The two brothers almost laughed out loud, the position was so ridiculous.

"Then we are both in the wrong place - my brother as well as I! You must pardon our ignorance of your customs. I saw the men and women sitting apart, but never imagined the widowers had a particular place for themselves. Tell us, pray, where we can sit to be among unmarried fellows like ourselves."

"Nay, my dear sir, remain where you are. The love-feast will soon be over. Brother Daniel, who leaves us to-morrow, to help Brother Joseph among the Kaffres, has only to take leave of us before we disperse."

While he was speaking, the whole assembly arose, and one among them stepped forward. He first advanced to the Sisters, and shook hands with each one; then passing over to the Brothers, the parting kiss was given and received. And he who thus bade farewell, ere he followed Brother Joseph, to share his struggles and hardships, far away from civilized life, was the identical awkward, ungainly-looking Brother who, in the morning, had made such an unsuccessful attempt at riding.

There is always an intolerable feeling of moral defeat when we see a man, whom we have regarded with contempt rise into importance by his own merit. A noble mind at once acknowledges the fact, but a mean spirit feels only resentment and spite, with a sense of defeat.

Something like a feeling of shame came over Alexander, as he closely regarded the man whom he had inwardly despised, but who now seemed like a hero in his eyes.

Seated at the table, opposite to him were the young sisters and pupils belonging to the educational department, and among them Adele, seated not far from Carmen. As Alexander casually looked up, he met Carmen's sparkling eyes, which seemed to cast on him a look of triumph, as if she understood his feeling of humiliation which this moment brought to him as a consequence of his contemptuous manner in the morning. He thought he could clearly read in her expression what she fain would have said: "You may perhaps ride well, and he cannot; you were not afraid to stop the wild horse and save the child's life; but would you have the courage to undertake what he has been appointed to do?" As their eyes met, she returned his glance unflinchingly and firmly, but he could not prevent his eyes from falling before hers.

Meanwhile Brother Daniel had, in his rounds of leave-taking, approached those near to Alexander. When he reached the latter he hesitated a moment, having recognized the person who had come to his assistance in need, and a flush of embarrassment suffused his gentle, almost effeminate, countenance. But Alexander, bending down quickly, pressed a kiss on the man's cheek, saying heartily: "Farewell, and good luck go with you! Believe me, I thoroughly admire your courage."

The Brother looked at him in surprise, and answered: "Thank you very much, sir!" and passed on.

When Alexander again looked toward Carmen, her eyes were moist with unshed tears.

"How beautiful that girl is!" thought he. "What an independent, frank spirit speaks from her eyes; what a lovely expression hovers around her mouth! She is like a dazzling star among these quiet people, - as if she had strayed away from her own orbit and found herself here, - so little does she seem fitted to her surroundings in the little circle in which she moves. I wonder if she is happy here. A large-hearted, generous nature cannot be content to submit to all these restrictions. No, she resists them. I saw that to-day. But she will never become like the others, and pass her life, in quiet submission, by the side of a man such as

Brother Daniel, for instance."

The leave-taking of the Brother being ended, the congregation received the general blessing and dispersed. The moment had now come when Frau von Trautenau and her sons must part from Adele, and many were the tears shed on the occasion.

The night grew late; the lamp was lighted in Agatha's room. Presently a gentle tapping was heard on the door, answered by a kindly "Come in."

Carmen entered; and when Agatha, raising her eyes, recognized the girl, she put aside her spectacles, and said gently: "Come nearer, dear Sister; I was expecting you." She drew up a chair, but Carmen put it aside, and kneeling by Sister Agatha's side, said:

"No, Sister, let me remain here and hear what you have to say, for you are going to chide me - I am sure of it."

"Carmen, do you believe I love you?" she inquired.

"Surely," answered the girl, quickly. "More than any one else here."

"Then you know that my heart grieves when I cannot feel satisfied with you," continued the Sister. "Why are your thoughts constantly dwelling on worldly things, and why do you allow yourself to be overcome with pride, instead of putting your mind on serious matters, and being more humble?"

"You are angry with me, Sister Agatha, because I did not tell from what distant land I came. That is not such a dreadful crime," said Carmen, cheerfully.

The serious countenance of the Sister grew yet more grave, and she looked severely at the kneeling figure.

"Have you, then, not thought of the text for to-day?" she asked reprovingly,

Carmen flushed up quickly; she tried to compose herself, but was for a moment at a loss what to say. She had during the past day been through such new experiences; whereas, heretofore, every day had been pretty much the same.

Sister Agatha waited patiently for Carmen to become calmer. At last, when she seemed to have forgotten her confusion about the text, Agatha said: "Now tell me the watchword."

When the maiden's eyes turned to the usual place for the motto, her thoughts seemed to cease wandering, and she repeated the verse correctly:

"'Feed Thou Thy people with Thy staff.'"

"Remember, my Sister, the purport of those words. 'Thy people' are those who belong to Him; 'with Thy staff' means, with the support of His strength. Carmen, how can the Lord guide you with His staff, if you do not bow your will before Him, and try to curb your pride?"

Carmen, as she knelt, had rested her elbows on Sister Agatha's lap, and thus supported her head on her hands, while she gazed into the speaker's face, thinking earnestly of what she said.

"Do you call it pride, and are you vexed with me because I would not tell to strangers what was indifferent, or perhaps amusing, to them? Oh, Sister Agatha, is it necessary that we expose ourselves to the derision of the world? We do not serve God by doing that. And when you speak of pride, is it not that very feeling which leads you to boast of our having come from so many and such distant lands? Do you not wish to demonstrate by that means how your faith has penetrated into all parts of the world? That is, after all, pride under the garb of humility."

Sister Agatha was deeply touched, and remained silent for a moment; then rising hastily, she said with a stern manner: "Do not confuse trifles with grave subjects. All that we do, even the weakest, is for the Lord's glory and praise, and not our own. What matter if the world scorns us? If we are the Lord's, He is with us, and we care for naught else. Search your heart, dear Sister, that you neglect not the salvation of your soul. Accept for yourself a helper and guide, so that your feet may not stray from the right path. There is one, whom I know, is now ready to offer himself to you, than whom none is, more steadfast in the faith. Brother Jonathan Fricke, the faithful friend of your father, honors you most highly when he desires to have you for his wife. To-day he explained to me his wishes on the subject; and the elders, to whom I have spoken, give their cordial consent to the alliance."

At Agatha's words Carmen grew deathly pale, and listened with wide-open eyes. When the Sister ceased speaking, she sprang up, and turning from the gentle eyes which sought hers, said passionately:

"But I will not have him for my husband!"

"Carmen, my dear, you will not have Jonathan for your husband? You do not know what you are saying," cried Agatha.

"Yes, I do, Sister Agatha," answered Carmen, quickly, her large lustrous eyes gleaming with a dangerous light. "Do you know how you feel when you come in contact with a reptile, a snake? When I was a little girl, on my father's plantation, I saw one day, under an aloe-tree, what I thought was a green twig; and when I grasped it, it was a cold, clammy snake, which, in a moment, twined itself around my arm. I could not scream for terror; but Sarah, my mother's faithful slave, saw it. She tore the viper from my arm, and flung it far away, among the bushes. Sister Agatha, when Brother Jonathan comes near me, I feel the same shiver go through, and the same feeling of horror almost paralyzes my limbs. I could not endure to have him near me always. I could not say to him, 'My husband' - no, not for all the world!"

Carmen grew more and more excited as she went on.

"Perhaps not for all the world," interposed Agatha; "but for your own salvation you must do it. Do not thrust the safety of your soul from you in this way. As Brother Jonathan's wife, you will be a partaker of his holy life and good works. We are not put into this world to please ourselves, but to further the progress of the kingdom of God."

"Oh, Sister Agatha, believe me, I will become a nurse for the sick, and bear all the hardships and trials of such a vocation; only spare me - spare me this one thing! I cannot give myself to Brother Jonathan. You must not - you dare not require it of me!" cried the girl, bursting into tears.

"No, Carmen, I will not compel you, although it grieves me for your sake," said Agatha. "Go, now, and on your knees examine your heart, lest you may refuse that which is intended for your greatest good." And kissing Carmen, she dismissed her.

The hours wore on, and still Sister Agatha remained lost in thought, wondering what new ideas had been put into that young head. "Perhaps she was right. Vanity and pride! How frightful the words sound! We never know ourselves as well as we do others; so, after all, the child has given me a good lesson. I must look into my own heart more thoroughly, and be more severe with myself, before I presume to advise and guide other people. Lord, help me to a right knowledge of my duty to Thee!"

She extinguished the light, and sought repose from her anxieties.

CHAPTER V.

A week passed quietly by, and the excitement caused by Brother Daniel's departure had given place to the usual monotonous religious routine. During this time things had gone badly with Adele. Self-control and obedience were things entirely new to her, and she felt by no means attracted towards the young girls about her, always excepting Carmen. The predilection which her mother had shown for the latter had quickly communicated itself to the daughter, and Carmen, in return, feeling that she could never be sufficiently grateful to Frau von Trautenau for her kindness, showed every possible favor to Adele. This young lady's naturally vivacious and merry disposition, which was not at all subdued by the calm seriousness which surrounded her, proved a great source of amusement to Carmen. She gladly reciprocated the warm affection lavished upon her by the petted heiress, and every letter which reached Wolmershain teemed with the pleasure the two friends took in each other's society. Adele told how Carmen had passed her eighteenth birthday, and now wore pink instead of red; how Carmen had undertaken to teach some of the English classes, and how all the girls loved their new teacher, etc., etc.

Carmen's natural cheerfulness had not been disturbed by the communication Sister Agatha had made to her in regard to Brother Jonathan. The morning after, Sister Agatha asked if she had considered the matter well, and prayed over it; to which Carmen answered in the affirmative, but persisted in her positive refusal; to which Brother Jonathan submitted with apparent calmness. If he felt at all mortified, he certainly exerted immense self-control, for he seemed the same as usual, and his voice was clear and firm; so that Agatha felt sure that it was only his great unselfishness which had prompted him to entertain the idea.

His profession took him frequently to the Sisters' house, but when there he had intercourse only with the nurses and patients. 'Tis true he now came oftener than formerly, and at more irregular hours, on the plea of looking after this or that which he had forgotten; but as he, with silent tread, passed along through the halls, he seldom met any of the Sisters, and Carmen never.

To-day had been rainy and wet, but towards evening the sky cleared up, and Carmen led little Frieda home from the school-house. On her return she took a roundabout path, and slackened her usually fleet steps to enjoy the fresh, balmy spring air. She passed into a lonely lane, bordered on either side with beautiful gardens, whose hedges were unfolding their first blossoms, filling the air with sweetest perfume. As she stooped to pick some lovely violets which peeped up from the wayside, she, all at once, felt as if some one was standing behind her, although no footfall had reached her ear. She raised herself hastily from her stooping posture, and as she did so, felt a man's strong arm passed around her, and in another second she was pressed violently to his breast. She strove to cry out for help, but voice and tongue failed her, as she turned and met Brother Jonathan's burning glance; and there seemed to thrill through her, under the touch of his arm, the same creeping, numbing horror that she felt when the snake coiled about her arm. But how changed he looked! His whole countenance seemed lighted up by a new expression, and eager, passionate words poured from his lips.

"Carmen, so young, so warm-hearted, why can you not respond to a love which is offered to you with all the intensity of a true heart? You see in me only the grave, elderly man who wants you for his wife, and therefore you reject him. But, Carmen, under this calm exterior you will find an ardent lover, who desires to win you, that he may make for you a heaven on earth, and fill your life with such unutterable bliss as you have never dreamed of. Oh, Carmen, do not say me nay; but lay your lovely head upon my breast, and believe that my heart throbs wildly and deeply for you only. Look in my eyes, and let the love you read there serve to kindle a like feeling in you. Have you forgotten that we must love one another, we Brothers and Sisters? Give me your love, then, my darling, and say you will be mine!"

Rendered powerless to move by his pitiless embrace, she seemed like a little bird doomed to death by the irresistible fascination of a serpent. Quickly, passionately, his hot breath scorching her bloodless lips, he kissed her again and again. With a sudden powerful effort she tore herself from his arms, retreated a few steps, and turning on him a countenance ablaze with scorn and indignation, she cried:

"Back, villain! How dare you venture to insult me thus? Approach one step nearer, and I will cry out so that heaven and earth will fly to my succor."

She stood before him, so proud and haughty, so intensely excited, that he dared not venture farther.

"I will not approach you again, Carmen, if it displeases you; and forgive my violence just now," he pleaded earnestly. "But promise to give yourself to me, Carmen; you are not by nature cold; you will, you must return my love. Let me teach you what real happiness is; you may imagine it, but you cannot come near the reality."

The girl was silent; this antipathy to Jonathan was as old as her memory. In Jamaica he had been an object of aversion to her, yet she could give no definite reason for this deeply-rooted dislike. Every one spoke so highly of him that she often blamed herself for not feeling more kindly towards one who enjoyed the respect and esteem of the whole community. His piety and temperate habits, his humility and devotion to his work, were conspicuous even here. Of late, he had been particularly friendly towards Carmen, which seemed a very natural thing, he having been such an old friend of her father's. But his increased kindness only awoke a greater dislike in the girl, so that she tried in every way to escape an avowal from him of his feelings. She did not consider her refusal to marry him a matter of much importance, as she concluded his offer had arisen only from a desire to transfer his friendship from the father to the daughter. His unexpected outburst of passion alarmed her, although in her childish innocence, she did not fully understand why she felt so deeply insulted. The thought that he had given her a love which she could not return made her fearful of hurting his feelings in some way beyond her comprehension, and she endeavored to subdue her anger sufficiently to answer him.

"Forgive me if I wound you, Brother Jonathan, but I cannot help it. I do not love you as you desire, and I neither deserve nor wish that you should have such a warm feeling for me."

"Carmen, you surely cannot mean what you say. I have taken you by surprise. Calm yourself, and do not make this a final decision." He attempted to approach her again, but the maiden shrank back from him in terror.

"I cannot do otherwise," she said firmly. "Now let me, I pray, go on my way in peace. Sister Agatha must be waiting for me."

At the mention of the Sister's name, Jonathan gave an anxious glance at Carmen. It flashed on his mind what fearful consequences might result from his conduct. He remembered the law of the Brotherhood, which required that the members must report the slightest departure from strict morality in any one of their number, so that the delinquent be reprimanded and excluded once or twice from the monthly celebration of the Communion. Should he give evidence of repentance, and return to the right path, he might be restored to his usual privileges; but if he should not acknowledge his fault, he must absent himself from the society of others, and, in an extreme case, be banished from the Brotherhood.

Brother Jonathan, heretofore so strict, and spotless in his reputation, to be publicly accused and admonished! What an appalling example of fallen greatness!

At the mention of Agatha's name, he endeavored to resume his habitual calmness. He passed his hand over his eyes, as if to blot out the remembrance of the passion which yet burned within him, and gradually regained, in voice and manner, a more collected mien.

"You have seen, dear Sister, how our passions sometimes get the mastery over us, and how vain are our efforts to subdue them, even though we have devoted ourselves to a religious life!" said he, in an humble tone. "If you cannot give me your love, you can at least be silent about my feeling towards you, and forget what has just occurred, and for which I shall ask pardon from Heaven."

Carmen looked at him, with a feeling of pity. She had brought so much trouble to this man that the thought of it did much towards dissipating her ill-will towards him. With tears in her eyes, she said: "Be easy about that, Brother Jonathan. I will not betray you. Forget this hour, as I will try to forget it."

Then turning away, she hurried, as fast as her feet would carry her, to the safe shelter of the Sisters' house.

From this time forth, Carmen's peace of mind was gone. Her aversion to Jonathan was outweighed by her fear of him. His hot, ardent nature had broken bounds so violently and ungovernably that she could not feel at all sure it was so quickly subdued. A deep sense of desolation, came over her. Her mother, lying in the grave, far away on a sea-girt island, under a tropical sun; her father, in all likelihood murdered, and buried in some foreign land; and she living among strangers, with whom she found it utterly impossible to feel any congeniality! She avoided Brother Jonathan, and he seemed to shun her no less assiduously. He had absented himself from one Communion; explaining his conduct by expressing an unusual sense of his own unworthiness. His calculations were well made: Carmen pitied him sincerely on account of the deep remorse he seemed to feel. How could her pure mind imagine it was all hypocrisy! In the house where he lived with the other unmarried Brothers, he maintained the same pious, serious demeanor as heretofore. His patients received the same care and attention as formerly, but he looked haggard and care-worn, and Thomas, his faithful attendant, whom he had brought with him from the New World, would often hear him groan heavily in the night, as if some secret grief preyed on his mind.

Carmen could not witness his misery unmoved. Since the unfortunate incident connected with him, her life among the Sisters had become doubly oppressive to her. Like a welcome release from her unpleasant surroundings came a request from Frau von Trautenau that Sister Agatha would permit Adele and her dear Carmen to spend Whitsuntide with her at Wollmershain; an invitation which Agatha gladly accepted for her pupils.

Wollmershain was a large, beautiful estate, which, upon the death of its owner, had become the joint property of Adele and her brothers; and Frau von Trautenau had resided there since her widowhood, and proposed to continue doing so until one of her sons should buy his sister's and brother's portion and assume the management of it. The relations between Frau von Trautenau and her step-son had always been of the most happy and agreeable kind; he

M. CORVUS

honored and loved his step-mother, who had brought him up with the greatest possible care and affection; and she, in return placed implicit confidence in his opinions and advice, making him her chief counsellor since her husband's death.

Into this beautiful home-life Carmen now entered, as if into a new world. Whereas, the affection between the Brothers and Sisters in the "community" had always appeared to her in the austere light of a duty, here it seemed like a natural impulse, springing spontaneously from the depths of warm and loving hearts.

In all the arrangements of the house and grounds, the idea of the beautiful, in connection with the comfortable and useful, was everywhere prominent.

The lofty, well-lighted rooms, adorned and furnished with elegant simplicity; the smooth green lawns, bordered with lovely flowers of every hue; the magnificent avenues of grand old trees, and the innumerable, lovely little nooks to be found here and there in the park, all breathed a charm which reminded Carmen of what she dimly remembered about her father's plantation and hacienda in Jamaica.

Alexander and Hans were also at home for the holidays; and while Adele rambled with the latter through park and garden, Carmen, who shyly avoided Alexander, was entertained by her hostess, to whose warm motherly nature the girl was attracted with genuine, childlike heartiness. It was indeed her society, more than anything else, which contributed to Carmen's happiness at Wollmershain, for she felt embarrassed in this new kind of life; and the remarks which her peculiar dress occasioned were especially annoying. To avoid being conspicuous, she had already laid aside the white cap; but her beauty, enhanced by the coils of glossy hair which crowned her queenly little head, was so remarkable, so foreign-looking and striking, that she seemed like some rare exotic which, in all the luxuriance of its loveliness, had been transplanted from the land of palms to our colder soil. There was in her manner an odd mixture of pride and humility, dignity and modesty, which gave her all the reserve of a woman and the winsomeness of a child. Perhaps it was the knowledge of the fact that the peculiarities of the Sisters elicited so much ridicule from the world that caused her to use her pride as a defence and a weapon, when in company with any one save Frau von Trautenau. She always seemed ready to do battle with Alexander, and yet he had never by word or deed given cause for such a feeling.

"She is full of pluck and mettle like a thoroughbred horse!" said old General von Bergen, who, with his daughter and his adjutant, had come up from the barracks on a visit. "It is a pleasure to provoke her; her eyes light up so. Pohlen," he said, turning to the adjutant, "you seemed to be unfortunate in your remarks to her during dinner; those lovely lips curled as scornfully as if you had seriously offended her, and her great eyes glowed like fire, as she looked away off, over your head."

The gentleman addressed laughed as if amused. "And yet I only ventured on some complimentary speeches. I asked if all the Creoles were as beautiful as herself. That was surely flattering enough, and I think this little Moravian ought, by this time, to possess some of the humility they pride themselves so much on, and not toss her head so haughtily and look at me so contemptuously."

The gentlemen were comfortably smoking in the veranda, after dinner; and Alexander, who sat on the steps, half hidden by a large syringa-bush in full bloom, flushed deeply at Pohlen's words. In a sharp tone of reprimand, he said:

"My friend, Creole is a term which is not at all agreeable to some people; for the rest, flattery is often another name for insult; perhaps the young lady considered yours as such."

"Do you think so?" drawled out Pohlen. "That is altogether a new thing to me. A lady of higher quality would at least have known how to receive homage offered to her; and a second time I will not put up with a rebuff from this Moravian girl, but will treat her as she does me."

Alexander colored with anger, and his blood boiled. It was only by a powerful effort that he controlled himself sufficiently to answer in a tolerably calm voice:

"A lady of higher quality? Higher quality presupposes greater merit, and you will do well to bear in mind, Herr von Pohlen, that this lady is my mother's guest, and, as such, is under my most special protection. Any mortifi=-cation or insult inflicted on her is also inflicted on me."

"Gentlemen, I beg the conversation may not become serious, but retain the bantering tone in which I began it. Let what has been said lead to nothing unpleasant," interrupted the general, in a pacifying manner. "Herr von Pohlen will, of course, remember what he owes to the inmates of this hospitable mansion. You two fortunate knights must vie with each other as to who shall win the favor of this young maiden, who is as beautiful as a dream. For myself, I lament nothing so much as my sixty years, which prevent me from entering the lists with you."

Alexander rose as the old man finished speaking, and as he passed down the steps, said:

"If agreeable, let us find the ladies now, General; they are, I think, awaiting us on the lawn."

He paused abruptly, for at the foot of the steps stood Carmen, as if irresolute whether to advance or withdraw. She had evidently heard the foregoing conversation, for she was very pale and trembled slightly. The young officer descended quickly toward her, as she raised her head, and calmly waited for him to pass. As he came up to where she stood, she whispered softly:

"I thank you!" and a gentle glance from the beautiful black eyes thrilled him with pleasure. Then seeing the other gentlemen preparing to descend also, her face became suffused with blushes.

"I came to find a cushion for Frau von Trautenau," she remarked confusedly.

"Allow me, Fraulein Carmen, to take it to my mother," said Alexander, coming to her assistance; and he ran back, upstairs, as she hastened away.

Games were now arranged on the lawn, and Fraulein von Bergen, a merry maiden, soon had every one actively engaged in them. There were familiar ones, which Carmen had often played at school with the day-pupils; but how different they seemed here, when the gentlemen took part in them! Carmen could never have been as unrestrained as the general's daughter; but she laughed merrily and enjoyed it all, contenting herself with allowing Adele to catch her, and carefully avoiding any contact with the others.

After a while a drop of rain fell, then another, and at last a hard shower drove the party from the open air into the drawing-room; but the spirit of merriment had been aroused, and sitting down quietly was not to be thought of.

"Come, papa, lead out your war-horse to the front!" urged the general's daughter; and the old gentleman good-naturedly seated himself at the piano and began thrumming the one, solitary piece he could play - a lively galop. Herr von Pohlen seized Fraulein von Bergen, Hans his sister, and the two couples went whirling through the mazes of the dance.

Carmen looked on with sparkling eyes; a bright flush of happiness colored her cheek, her little foot involuntarily beat time, and her lithe form swayed to and fro with a dreamy, rhythmical movement.

"Will you not dance also?" asked Alexander, close beside her.

"Oh, I would like to, above all things!" she replied with a lovely smile, her eyes still fixed on the dancers. "How delightful it must be to whirl around so!"

"Will you not try it with me, Fraulein Carmen?" he urged pleadingly.

"I cannot dance; at least, not like that!" she returned, turning her beaming countenance towards him.

"Oh, it is very easily learned; just trust yourself to my guidance. Put your hand on my shoulder, if you please, and with my arm I will hold you firmly as we move around;" saying which, he proceeded to put his arm about her waist. But she drew back, and gave him a horrified look. As yet, no man's arm had encircled her - except Brother Jonathan's, during that one dreadful moment of her life.

"I cannot do it - no, it is quite impossible!" she stammered.

"Then you must pardon me for making the attempt," said Alexander, and bowed coolly.

"Refused!" whispered Pohlen, mockingly, when he stopped dancing, for he had seen Alexander's defeat.

"Yes; but as she knows *how* to refuse, it is perhaps more to be appreciated than when others accept," he replied.

When the family separated for the night, and Carmen had as usual given her hand to her hostess, Adele, and Hans, she hesitated a second, and then, with a burning blush mantling her cheek, extended her hand to Alexander.

Heretofore she had persistently avoided him; but to-day he had proved himself her friend and protector, and she felt that some reparation was due him for her rudeness in the past.

As she held out the little hand, and wished him "Good-night," she gave him a pleading glance, as if to say, "Do not be angry with me!"

His countenance lighted up with surprise and pleasure. Her eyes, so fascinating when flashing with indignation, now seemed irresistible when moistened by a gentler emotion; and as he looked into their dark, unfathomable depths, he felt as if he would like to gaze forever. But her eyes fell before his ardent glance, and bowing low over the proffered hand, he kissed it respectfully, feeling as honored as if a queen had allowed him the privilege.

From this night Carmen's intercourse with Alexander assumed a much more friendly character; but was, of course, very brief, as only two more days remained ere the pleasant party at Wollmershain would be broken up, and Adele and Carmen return to their duties.

CHAPTER VI.

"Dear old home! At last I see you again!" exclaimed a lonely traveller, as he stood leaning on his staff, and viewed the scene before him. He took off his hat, and folded his hands as if in silent thanksgiving. Footsore and weary he seemed to have paused here to refresh himself with the sight of a place so dear to him.

There lay the little Moravian settlement, bathed in the soft glow of a summer sunset. Bright clouds reflected a golden radiance on the pointed roofs and windows, and trembled on the bosom of the little stream, which, with gentle murmur, flowed at the stranger's feet. The dark shadows of the hills extended down into the valley opening on his right, and from the evening mist peeped out the old mill, which he remembered so well. On the meadows around the alder-pond, the evening fog wreathed itself into fairy forms, and the fragrance of new-mown hay was borne on the breeze.

It was a lovely, peaceful picture, and seemed to affect the man very deeply. And yet he had been in the midst of far grander, more sublime, more beautiful scenery than this! He had crossed the ocean, and revelled in the contemplation of its grandeur. He had dwelt under tropical skies, palms and magnolias shading his home, and the boundless riches of the West Indian world poured out at his feet. He had looked upon the sacred waters of the Ganges, and gazed in wonder on the temples of Benares; had traversed "the home of the snows" on the Himalayas; and the ice crown of the Dhawalagiri had frowned on him, gigantic and mystical, as he sojourned in the green valleys below, rich with banana-groves and rice fields. He had wandered over Mongolian steppes, and the stars of heaven had watched over him as he lay in the tent of the nomad; but never, through all, had the yearning for home been quenched within him.

"Home!" How the word recalls long-lost memories! The mother's gentle smile, the father's loving word, as when, in childhood's happy hours, we sought the beloved shelter at evening, and betook ourselves to innocent slumbers; and, although the child grows to be the gray-haired man, yet the sweet memories of peace and love never fade from his heart. What changes life brings to us! Thirty years ago this worn, weary traveller emigrated to the New World. Then he was young, courageous, filled with all the bright hopes which a new life spread out before him. What happiness he had known since then; what sorrow he had passed through; and ah, what guilt and remorse he had borne!

And now he was back again - the tall, erect form so bowed down. Was it sorrow, guilt, or exhaustion from the journey? The once sunny locks were white as the snow on the mountains; in the large blue eyes alone there were still some signs of his former self remaining. "Here is the dear old place at last!" he murmured to himself, and his bosom heaved with suppressed emotion. The longer he gazed, the more difficult he found it to control his feelings, until finally he gave way, and wept like a child.

Meanwhile the brilliant hues of sunset had faded away, and with the approaching shadows of night the wind rose and played around the stranger's hoary head.

"It must be about nine o'clock now, the hour for evening prayer, and everything will go on just as in the old days, for there is nothing to create a change here. I will go in, and ask if my child yet lives; and if so, there may be one to rejoice at my return." Thus soliloquizing, he put his hat on again, slung his wallet over his shoulder, and supporting himself on his stout staff, approached the house. Very few changes had occurred since he had left. A few new houses had been erected, but the old ones remained unaltered, even the one where he had formerly lived. He had inherited it from his father, and had carried on the linen trade there until he left with his first wife for the New World.

The congregation were returning from the chapel. Here and there a group would gather before one or other of the dwellings, to enjoy the mild summer night; and as the old man passed along he greeted a Brother or a Sister, and they returned it kindly, but like strangers. No one recognized him, although many looked after him curiously as he staggered feebly on towards the Sisters' house.

"That is not the Brothers' house, dear Brother," said a young man, addressing him.

"Yes, I know it. But I know where I am going," he replied, as if pleased to find the different roads so familiar to him. Then he pulled the bell at the Sisters' door, and requested to speak with Agatha.

He was ushered into the sitting-room, and as Sister Agatha entered, recognized her at the first glance.

"Sister, does Carmen Mauer still live, and is she here?" he asked, trembling with intense suspense.

The speaker must once have been a very handsome man. He bore evidences of it to-day, although deep sorrow and bodily as well as mental suffering had set its seal on his face and left deep furrows there. The burning suns of many climes had bronzed his skin, so that the large, clear blue eyes shone forth like stars.

Agatha looked at him inquiringly, and the more she looked the more perplexed she became. "Carmen lives here in this house," she answered, at length. "Can it be possible that you are -"

"Brother Mauer, who you have thought was dead ages ago," he replied falteringly.

"Heaven be praised!" cried Agatha, and sank into a chair. The surprise was almost too great for her; but regaining her self-control in a measure, she cordially pressed his outstretched hand, and led him to a seat, saying: "Let me go and bring Carmen at once, and you shall clasp your child to your heart without delay."

CHAPTER VII.

Sister Agatha lost not a moment. "Rejoice, dear Carmen," she said. "A Brother has just arrived who brings intelligence that your father still lives!" And with a most unwonted excitement in her manner, she led Carmen to the door of the sitting-room. Tremblingly the girl entered, and saw by the clear light of the lamp an old, bent man who had, at this moment, no power to rise to his feet, but could only stretch out his longing arms to his dearly-loved daughter. The next moment she lay sobbing on his breast. The child had not forgotten the sweet expression of those eyes, and she read in the dear features the fact that she was not an orphan.

"Father! my dear, dear father!"

His eyes bedewed her brow with tears of joy as with loving tones he murmured again and again: "My child! my darling!" In her warm embrace he again felt the happiness which had been denied him during so many weary years. After a little while, he gently turned her face up towards him, and examined her features.

"Just like Inez! You are your mother over again, as I first saw her under the palms and fell in love with her. In you I have found both of my lost ones!" he said, and he smiled through happy tears.

"You will stay with me now, dear father? You will never leave me again?" she asked anxiously.

"Yes, I will remain here, Carmen, in the dear old home, where I have come, a worn-out pilgrim to rest."

"Poor father! how much you must have endured, working so far away from us all! You have been all alone, no one to succor or help you; and nothing has been heard of you for so long; all efforts to find you have proved useless," said Carmen, as she lovingly stroked the withered cheek. "You had vanished so utterly that they all gave you up as dead; only my heart could never believe it. Why have you never sent us any tidings?"

"I did indeed send some, my child, but they never reached you. I was on the banks of the Ganges at the time, but shortly afterwards I went farther into the country, towards the north, attempting to penetrate a defile in the Himalayas. There the savages seized me and made me a slave. For years I have served in the most menial and degrading capacity; my tired back often bruised with their lashes, and only the stony ground on which to rest. At length I escaped on horseback, and succeeded in reaching the Mongolian steppes. There I have been wandering about, with various tribes, for two years; have tended their flocks and performed the commonest labor; all the time trying to teach them the Gospel. But only the spirit of unrest reigned within me, and an intense longing impelled me to turn my face homeward. So I took my staff and passed on foot through Siberia, into Russia, begging my way from door to door. I, who possess hundreds of thousands! Finally I reached Sarepta, ragged and barefooted, and almost dead from exhaustion. There the Brothers wanted me to remain with them, to be nursed and cared for; but this uncontrollable longing did not suffer me to tarry. After reaching Europe I felt as if I was on the threshold of home, and I grew more impatient than ever. I obtained a loan of money from the Brothers, and was thus enabled to ride the rest of the journey, and get some suitable clothing; but I sickened on the road and was forced to lay up in a Polish town, where I remained until nearly all my money was gone. Afterwards I was again obliged to travel on foot - and here I am. Now all will go well, since I am again at home," he concluded, smiling contentedly at the last thought.

Sister Agatha had, meanwhile, brought refreshments for the weary old man. What a heart-felt joy, this first meal with his daughter in the old familiar room! And how much he had to relate, while regaling himself, of wonders and adventures in distant lands! It was very late when, strengthened by the good cheer, and comforted by the presence of his child, he bade good-night to Carmen and Sister Agatha, and betook himself to the lodging-house to seek repose.

* * * * * *

"Have you heard the news? Brother Mauer, whom we thought dead and buried, is here!" passed from lip to lip in the settlement the next morning. The wonderful event occupied every mind, and filled the Brothers and Sisters with amazement. But no one except Carmen had seen him as yet. He had slept until near noon, recovering some of his lost strength, and his daughter had sat quietly watching by him during the whole morning, so that his first waking glance might fall on her. Afterwards they took breakfast together in his room, each recounting the occurrences of the past years, and drawing happy plans for the future. He proposed to buy a house in the settlement, and Carmen should keep house for him, nothing but death ever separating them again.

Carmen's heart grew light as a bird. She was so delighted to have her father restored to her - so happy in the security of a love which would always shelter and protect her! It would shield her even against Brother Jonathan's love, which was so abhorrent to her; and she took counsel with herself whether or no it would be best to tell the old man all the terror she had suffered a short time before. Truly a promise of silence had been given; but ought she not to make her father an exception? She could not see clearly what was the right thing to do, and therefore resolved not to mention Jonathan at all.

The latter had gone on a short journey a few days previously, and she would thus have time to consider the matter, and wait for some quieter hour in which to make her disclosure.

In the afternoon, when service was held in the chapel, everybody hastened thither, intent upon seeing Brother Mauer, and hearing about his mission work and adventures. He sat among the widowers; devoutly singing, his eyes cast down, as if he felt that all eyes were gazing upon him.

When the hymn was ended, the principal elders and teachers came up to Mauer, greeting him with cordial hand-shakings, and leading him, with words of hearty welcome, to a more prominent seat, from which he could address the congregation. He bore himself with a firmer carriage to-day, and the dignity of his tall figure was more conspicuous than on the evening before. With a happy smile, he let his glance roam over the assembly of Brothers and Sisters, many of whom were unknown to him; indeed, the large majority were strange, yet he held each and all dear, as forming a part of his home surroundings. As he passed up the aisle, between the two elders who conducted him, the door of the chapel opened, and a tardy member entered. It was Brother Jonathan Fricke. His manner was even humbler than usual, and his eyes wandered restlessly around: perhaps he had heard of Brother Mauer's arrival, and was looking for him. In the centre of the aisle, which was filled with people, he met the three men. Jonathan's glance fell on the tall form of his old friend; he stretched out his hand, and said in a low voice:

"Do the dead rise, Brother Michael?"

Mauer shrank back at the words; and as he recognized the

speaker he grew deathly pale, his eyes dilated with an expression of horror, and he staggered forward.

"You here?" he asked hoarsely, and fell to the ground.

A general confusion ensued. It seemed but natural that the numerous greetings should have exhausted the over-weary traveller; and then the reunion with his old friend - it really had been too much for his strength, and the general feeling of sympathy grew deeper.

As they carried him away Carmen, followed to his room; and after long, untiring efforts the old man at last began to revive. Carmen begged that she might be left alone with him, so that when he came fully to himself he might be undisturbed and see no one but her, at the same time declining all offers of medical assistance from Brother Jonathan.

The girl seated herself by the bedside; and when her father opened his eyes, she noticed he looked anxiously around and then whispered:

"Child, who was that I last saw in the chapel and who spoke to me?"

"Do not trouble yourself, dear father. It was only your old friend, Jonathan Fricke," replied Carmen, soothingly, holding his hand in hers. She felt a shiver run through him as she mentioned the name.

"I did not know that he was here," he said with a groan.

"Can I help you in any way, dear father?" his daughter asked. "Are you in pain?"

He shook his head in reply, and lay quite still, with closed eyes. After a long time he looked again at Carmen in a troubled, sorrowful way, and sighed deeply. "Tell me about him," he murmured. "I thought he was still in Bethlehem, in America; how came he here, and how long has he been among you?"

She told him everything, save the one horrible incident that haunted her memory. His extreme agitation made her silent on that point. When she ceased speaking, all was silence in the apartment except the soft ticking of the clock. Occasionally a deeply drawn breath reached Carmen's ear; her father had turned his face to the wall, and was so quiet and motionless that she hoped he had fallen asleep from exhaustion. Suddenly he began to whisper to himself:

"The old, old story, which will never die! The idea of home, with its sweet repose and calm blessedness, was only a delusion after all!"

"What do you mean, father?" asked Carmen, bending over him. He closed his eyes wearily; and she noiselessly resumed her seat near him.

CHAPTER VIII.

The next day Mauer was still so entirely unnerved and overcome by the events of the day before that it was with the greatest difficulty he rose from the bed; and yet it was intolerable misery to remain there. All Carmen's persuasions were of no avail; he insisted on getting up and dressing; but was quite unable to leave the house, and required the most perfect quietness. She tried to divert his mind, by gentle, cheerful conversation, from the sad, gloomy thoughts which seemed to oppress him. It made the girl's tender heart ache, as she looked into his unutterably sad face, which only yesterday was beaming with such great joy.

At ten o'clock Jonathan came to pay a friendly visit. Fortunately Carmen, who was standing at the window, saw him coming across the street towards the house, and warning her father of the approaching visit, she could see how he started with terror at the information. But he soon controlled himself, and said in a resigned tone: "Let him come in. The sooner I get through all the meetings and greetings, the sooner I will have some rest. I must grow accustomed to seeing him, and I feel stronger to-day than yesterday. I have not seen him before, since your dear mother died, Carmen, and life has been one long unbroken sorrow since then." She made a movement to leave the room, so that the meeting between the friends should be private, but Mauer held her back and pleaded: "Stay with me, my child," as if he could not bear to have her out of his sight.

When Jonathan entered, he stood for a moment near the door, and his eyes sought to read the expression of the sick man's face. The latter sat with his head resting against the sofa-cushion, and his deep-sunken eyes fixed beseechingly on the visitor, as if saying, "Spare me!"

"Good-morning Brother Mauer!" cried Jonathan. "Are you feeling better to-day?" He held out his hand, into which the other placed his hesitatingly, and would have quickly withdrawn it had not Jonathan held it fast as he said:

"Let me feel your pulse. You are still very much fatigued, and your hand is as cold as ice."

"Thank you, Brother Jonathan," said the invalid; "I think perfect rest is the best remedy. I have borne many heavy burdens, dear Brother, which have weighed me down intolerably; and now that the Lord has led me home again, let your pity and sympathy be with me on account of all I have suffered."

"Certainly, Brother Michael; it cannot be otherwise. Your return has been a matter of great rejoicing with us all," replied Jonathan. "But I must give you a prescription, that you may gain your strength more quickly. Do not talk too much to-day; some time, later on, you must give us an account of your travels." With these words, he turned to Carmen with a searching look, as if to divine how far he might trust to her silence. She purposely avoided his eye, and remained standing at the window.

"I will make your father well again, if you will be kind to me in return," he said with emphasis.

Then she was compelled to turn and speak. This man ruled her, in spite of her dislike.

"If you can do anything for my father, Brother Jonathan, you will please not consider me in the matter, but do it for

God's sake and your own," she replied calmly.

He drew a chair up to the table, and, seating himself, wrote a prescription which he handed to Carmen.

"Have that prepared at once, dear Sister," he said, "and give it to your father according to the directions; it will benefit him very much. You know, Brother Michael, my remedies are very powerful." A peculiar, sarcastic expression played around his mouth as he spoke, and Carmen, whose quick eye perceived it, wondered what he was ridiculing. Was it her anxiety about her father, or was it the old man's weakness? But it came and went like a flash, and he resumed his usual manner as he rose to leave, saying to Mauer: "Adieu, Brother. May the Lord keep you and give you a speedy recovery!"

"I will have the medicine prepared at once, father," said Carmen, heaving a sigh of relief as the door closed behind the physician. But when she looked at the old man, a chill of anguish struck through her heart, for she saw how he had clasped his hands before his face, to hide the big tears which were trickling between his fingers.

*   *   *   *   *   *

Many days passed quietly away after Jonathan's visit. Carmen's soothing, cheering influence seemed to have somewhat allayed her father's nervousness, and a calmer, more equable mood seemed to have come over him, as his state of health daily improved. But the nameless shadow of a hidden grief seemed to hang over him. For his wants he needed but little; self-denial and sacrifice had grown to be a second nature to him, his one earthly wish seeming to be to have a house where he and Carmen could live alone together; but as regards others, he was open-handed and generous to help wherever it was needed. It was a very difficult matter to find just the right dwelling to suit his taste, so he finally concluded to build, renting in the meantime a comfortable suite of apartments for himself, while Carmen continued to live as heretofore in the Sisters' house; giving the smaller children a few hour's instruction, and passing the rest of the day with her father. She had regained all her vivacity of manner, for she considered her dear father her protector and support; little guessing that it was, in reality, quite the contrary, as he looked to her as his stay on which to lean. When alone with him, she allowed her naturally gay humor to have full sway, and he would smile contentedly when he heard her exquisite voice warbling forth, now a hymn, now a Spanish love-song, or when he saw her feet, as if inspired, try a half-forgotten Spanish dance, which seemed like a greeting to him from that tropical world where he had loved and suffered. Sometimes she would caress him with pretty, fascinating ways, as if her heart longed to lavish on him all the tenderness which had been gathering intensity during all the long years of separation.

"You are so like Inez! Gay and merry, like her," he would say with emotion, his eyes beaming with love. Thus she would succeed in charming away, for a few moments at least, the shadow which rested ever on his brow; and this success gave her a pure happiness she had never known before.

As the invalid grew stronger, every one hastened to visit him. The elders wanted a full account of his missionary work in Mongolia, and of the religious condition of the heathen in Bengal and the Himalayas; so Mauer was at last obliged to consent to give a public narration of his experiences. This could not fail to give him a certain degree of importance in the settlement, and it was suggested that he be elected to some public office. But he divested their minds of any such thought, and desired to be allowed a quiet and retired life; he was too modest and reserved to put himself forward at any time, and now anything like publicity was positively painful to him. Even when chatting socially with old friends, he displayed more or less shyness, and especially when Jonathan was present.

"A strange sort of friendship!" thought Carmen, as she noticed how her father never sought the doctor's society, but, on the contrary, seemed to tolerate his company with a kind of bitter endurance, as if he were in some secret way the master and Mauer the slave. Often, when Jonathan addressed him, he would suddenly change color and an involuntary expression of terror pass over his countenance; then the physician's words would assume a slightly scornful tone, and Mauer would humbly lower his eyes.

A few days after Jonathan's visit, he inquired how the prescribed medicine had affected him.

"Most beneficially," replied Mauer. "I feel stronger in every way."

"Just as I thought," said the other, smiling kindly. "I ordered fifteen drops, but now you can begin to take twenty; that will not be too strong - but positively not more, dear Brother."

Mauer looked up at him with an expression of keenest anguish, and gasped for breath; while Jonathan continued to smile at him.

No wonder Carmen thought, "What a strange sort of friendship!"

"It must be with my dear father as it is with me," she said to herself by way of explanation. "He recognizes the snake-like nature in Brother Jonathan, but dares not show it; and having been friends in early youth, he still loves him in spite of everything."

Weeks and months passed away. Mauer's house was in process of being completed, and he was constantly urging the workmen to have it ready for him as soon as possible, as he longed to be settled.

The plan had evidently been drawn on the same simple and spacious style of the hacienda in Jamaica, where Carmen's mother had lived. A wide, shady veranda was to extend all around, and a broad flight of steps to lead from it to the spacious grounds. Deep-seated windows were to open out on the garden, and elms instead of magnolias must shade them. But the veranda had to be given up, for, when the plan came under the observation of the elders, a committee called on Mauer and represented to him that such a thing would be a gross violation of the severe laws respecting the simple style of building used in the settlement, and would give cause for great offence. The inhabitants of the town must be content to live without ostentation and show, abiding by the general customs, and conducting themselves as humble members of the faith.

"Just to think: I, an old man, was going to set such a bad example and encourage foolish ideas!" said Mauer to his daughter, deeply mortified. "When one has been abroad, in different lands, as I have, much that belongs to the outside world clings to him when he gets home, and is never so noticeable as when he mingles once more with his brethren. The renouncing of our own will, and compliance with the wishes of others, has all to be learned over again."

"But," cried Carmen, impatiently, "they find impropriety in so many things here that one must needs give up thinking, in order to please them. The free spirit within us is so cramped and restricted that we cease to be individuals. It is surely not necessary to make automatons of ourselves if we wish to be good. No; we should choose the right of our own free will, because it is right; then we will not fail to do what is pleasing in the sight of God."

"Free spirit within us! What do you mean by that? We are so often the slaves of our own desires that our ideas of right and wrong get confused, and we lose our own souls thereby," returned her father, much agitated. "We should, therefore, never reject the path which our religion requires us to choose, but rather submit patiently, without arguing or any wish to rebel."

Thus the building which had been so beautifully planned, and with so much pleasure, turned out to be, when finished, just like all the others. But Carmen did not bear the frustration of their cherished hopes as calmly as the old man. Her visit to Wollmershain, although it had not given rise to any new tastes or dislikes regarding the home customs, had strengthened the long-buried desires which lay within her breast, and quickened her natural spirit of resistance to the existing state of things. Frau von Trautenau, as well as the style and manner of life at Wollm-ershain, was peculiarly congenial to her taste. Therefore, although the visit had never been repeated, she often lived it over again in her thoughts, and in speaking with her father always referred enthusiastically to persons and things there. One day, while describing the unrestrained and harmonious life of her new friends, the sound of trumpets playing a hymn came wafted in through the open door.

"Who is dead, Carmen?" asked Mauer, listening intently as he sat by the window. "Is that not the dirge of a bachelor Brother? I remember the air, as I do that of all our funeral hymns. How often, when suffering under my bondage as a slave, I have thought that at my death no music would be heard. But now I know that some day the trumpets will tell to the other brothers when the heart of old Mauer has ceased to beat."

"Oh, my father, you must not speak thus!" said Carmen, anxiously. "The person for whom the music is sounding is the bachelor Brother Christopher Yager, who died yesterday evening. He was the one who spoke in defence of our unmarried sisters in the general council; and now some one will have to be elected in his place."

This election followed immediately after the funeral, the elders casting votes for those they deemed most suitable for the position. The majority were in favor of Jonathan Fricke, who was received with universal satisfaction. No one was more pleased with the result than Sister Agatha, who always depended so much on him for advice. She felt that now, being able to entrust the affairs of her department to his wisdom and circumspection, his piety and brotherly love, was as if she handed her ship over to the guidance of a skilful and able captain. He received the honor with great humility, as a duty laid upon him from which he must not shrink, however unworthy he felt to bear the heavy responsibility. Yet in spite of all his apparent absence of pride, there was something about him which elicited the homage of the Sisters as they gave their promise to be willing to trust him with their confidence and follow his instructions.

CHAPTER IX.

Notwithstanding its being the month of September, a burning July heat prevailed, and, as a breath of wind would occasionally stir, great clouds of dust rose from the streets and lanes of the settlement. But in spite of the intense warmth of the sun, masons and carpenters were busily at work on Brother Mauer's house, which was located in a pleasant district on the outskirts of the town. From the windows on the first floor, which stood quite high from the ground, one could catch a fine view of the broad, sunny landscape. There was the green meadow-land, with its duck-pond, and beyond, round the road to the old mill in the valley, the steep path leading uphill to the graveyard, and finally, away off towards the south, great masses of dense forest, rising one above the other, covering the mountain-sides and shutting out all that lay beyond.

"So that will be your room dear father, and this one next to it mine," said Carmen, pleasantly, as she and the old man wandered about in the bright morning air over the grounds and through the partially finished building which was to be their home.

"How pretty it will be here, father! I will raise vines all around the windows, so that, in summer, a pretty shade will fall in the rooms; and even though we are not allowed to have any ornaments, a cabinet of books will be here, and by the window shall stand a table with a vase of flowers on it, while over there I will make a cosey little nook, like the one Frau von Trautenau has in her room. And then when evening comes, dear father, you shall sit by me, and tell me of the snow-capped Himalayas, and the wonders of the East Indian world. Or when the lamp is lighted, I will read to you, just as I did to Frau von Trautenau in her dear little nook."

"How often you speak of that lady, Carmen! Is she so very dear to you?" asked Mauer.

"Yes, very dear, father," she replied eagerly, and the warmth of her feelings betrayed itself in her countenance. "She was very, very kind to me; and with her, I, who was so lonely, felt how good it must be to look into a mother's eyes. I could always turn to her for sympathy and advice, feeling sure of being understood; and that was a great comfort to me, when I thought you never would return, father. She is not grave and austere, like our Sisters here, but is in all things noble and good; and even though she belongs to those who are outside in the world, yet anyone following her could not go wrong. The world!" she continued thoughtfully. "We are all of this world as long as we live. How can one set of people consider themselves so much better than the others?"

"We do not think ourselves better, child, but on a surer road to become so," interrupted the father. "And yet, even with us, there are no insurmountable barriers to keep us from straying into the by-paths which lead us away from the goal!" he added, with a sigh.

"Yes father," she said, with a fond smile. "That is just what I say. The right way and the wrong, cross each other everywhere in life, and we must ever be striving more and more to distinguish between them."

"May your heart never mislead you, child!" answered the old man with emotion. "One who has lived as long as I have, who has fallen and endeavored to make atonement, learns to mistrust the human heart."

"Listen, father; are not those shots?" exclaimed Carmen, excitedly, as from a distance were heard, at this moment, several dull reports of cannon. Closer and closer they came, mingled with the cracking of rifles; while from the borders of the forest, on the south, clouds of smoke ascended and curled in wreaths among the sombre pines, Mauer and his daughter went out and took up their station on the lawn, under an old linden-tree, from whence they could survey the scene at leisure. In the west the sky had become overcast; black clouds were gathering in threatening masses, and there was every indication of an approaching storm. Low rumblings of thunder reached the ear from time to time, together with the dull booming of artillery.

"What a number of shots! There must be something extra-ordinary going on!" exclaimed Carmen.

"There are troops practising over yonder in the forest," said one of the workmen, who had come out to satisfy his curiosity. "I hear they are quartered in the village on the other side of the woods."

Troops! What a startling circumstance! The other work-men, heretofore so quiet and diligent, stopped their labors, and gazed with surprise and curiosity towards the place from whence the smoke came. It was an almost unheard-of event for soldiers to be in this neighborhood. The Brothers, being conscienciously opposed to the use of fire-arms, had been exempted by the government from military duty; and many a one who left the settlement to go abroad had never seen a soldier.

Suddenly a flash was seen among the trees, followed by a roar, this time louder than before. Through the openings in the woods could be seen the gay colored uniforms, at first singly, then in groups; and finally in whole companies. Bayonets glittered in the sunlight; flags and standards waved, and bugles sounded from the distance.

"Oh, there they are! - the soldiers! How their weapons glitter!" cried Carmen, in delight. "How the cavalrymen gallop to and fro, and how their sabres shine! Just look, dear father, how splendid it is!"

"Yes, when no blood is being shed, one can look at it from a safe distance," said Mauer, soberly.

"Yet I don't know but what I would be a soldier if I were a man," replied the girl, excitedly. "It is, of course, a great sin to commit murder; but to fight for the fatherland, that must be a noble employment for a man. It seems to me, father, that a true man would stand in the fight and know no fear; who would throw himself into danger bravely, face it unflinchingly, and turn it aside by his prowess; under whose protection the weak seek for shelter; who has, with all his bravery, a gentle, tender heart, and a well-balanced mind - a man father, who, like the oak, sways not when weaker trees tremble in the storm."

"How is it possible that you know anything about soldiers?" asked Mauer, astonished at her enthusiasm.

"I met some of them at Wollmershain," she replied quickly.

"And were they such men as you describe?"

She hesitated a moment.

"No, not all of them. A man is not always what he ought to be."

"Wollmershain and Frau von Trautenau: between the two, your thoughts seem continually to wander, Carmen; everything you say springs from that subject, or leads back to it. You seem to have received very deep impressions; deeper, I am afraid, than is good for you."

She did not answer. Her gaze lingered on the scene before

her, watching the troops as they began to file off from the forest. Suddenly a large body of cavalry wheeled around from a screened corner in the woods, and the spectacle became more and more lively.

Carmen's face glowed with pleasure, and her eyes moved restlessly hither and thither, as if to take in the whole picture.

"I could sit here all day and watch them," she said. "It cannot be late, father, is it? Sister Agatha told me, when I came away this morning, that I must be back at eleven o'clock for something important."

"Eleven o'clock!" replied Mauer, looking at his watch. "Why, my child, it is almost twelve."

Carmen sprang up quickly. "Then I must go at once. What a pity! I want to stay so much. Adieu, dear father; I will be with you again this afternoon." She embraced and kissed the old man, and hurried away.

Meanwhile an unusual commotion prevailed in the Sisters' house. Whenever two met together there was whispering going on; the hands in the work-room rested oftener, and the heads were put together for a softly-spoken word; the eyes wandered about with inquiring glances, or watched the dial of the large clock that quietly ticked on in its usual monotonous fashion.

At last the hands pointed to the appointed hour, and eleven deliberate strokes chimed forth; whereupon the Sisters began to issue forth from every door, and betook themselves to the assembly-room.

Sister Agatha and the recently elected supervisor of the unmarried Sisters, Brother Jonathan, stood in the centre of the room, and near them the teachers and elders. When all had entered, and an expectant silence prevailed, Jonathan commenced an address to the congregation.

"As you probably already know, dear Sisters, a letter has been received from Brother Daniel, at Cape Colony, in which he informs us of his safe arrival in the country of the Caffres. He goes on to tell how he has met Brother Joseph Hubner and two other Brothers; and how a little band of devout Christians has begun to spring up, which with the Lord's help will further the work of rescuing souls from the darkness of heathenism, and win them to the truth. It is a glorious work which they have so piously undertaken, and blessed is every one who lends them a helping hand. Nothing is needed in their simple life, except one thing. They have no women to help to lighten the labor, and so Brother Joseph begs that his wife Christina, whom he left behind, may follow him; and Brother Daniel desires that we choose a helpmate for him, who may be sent out in company with Sister Christina. This request is very proper, and a beautiful field of work is thus opened for her who will become his wife, as she will be of the greatest assistance to her husband. We now wish, dear Sisters, to draw lots, and thereby decide which of you is called to this honor of helping our dear Brother in building up the faith; and we are prepared to recognize in the result a direct expression of the Lord's will, hoping it will be gladly and humbly obeyed."

When Jonathan had finished speaking, and arrangements were being made in the usual manner for the drawing, a buzz of excitement arose among the Sisters. Suspense was written on every face, but no one showed any fear. Custom and habit, which govern so completely the feelings of people, prevented the Sisters from feeling wounded or alarmed at being disposed of in this business-like manner; and therefore they allowed the ceremony to go on with cheerful resignation. Brother Jonathan laid down one after another of the drawn papers containing the names of the Sisters, while Sister Agatha at the same time let the blanks which she drew fall on the floor, waiting until she should turn up the one on which was written Brother Daniel's name. The spirit of humility with which it all was accepted, as coming from the Lord, stood written on these gentle faces which bore this trial so firmly. Not a single Sister trembled as her name was read by Brother Jonathan. About half the list had been called in this manner, when Jonathan, unrolling another paper, looked at it a moment in silence. He changed color, and involuntarily hesitated; but controlling himself, read in the same calm voice as before: "Carmen Mauer." He looked anxiously at Sister Agatha, whose trembling fingers tried to open the folded paper which she drew. After many futile efforts it was at last unrolled; she looked at it, and her hand sank slowly to her side as she read: "Brother Daniel Becker."

Hate or love, triumph or despair: which was it that stood so plainly written on Jonathan's face? For the moment he could not master his feelings.

"Sister Carmen Mauer!" The name passed from lip to lip, and echoed through the room. Carmen had endeared herself to everybody, although she was so different from them all. Her sweetness of manner had won their hearts, and her unselfishness and kindness had gained her many friends. "Carmen Mauer!" they called, repeatedly, but no answer came. Carmen was not present.

"Where is Sister Carmen Mauer?" asked Brother Jonathan, who had become sufficiently calm to speak; and something like a gleam of hope lit up his features.

"Here," replied a voice half-choked from swift running.

All eyes were turned towards the doorway where she stood; her cheeks rosy, and her large black eyes filled with wonder, as she glanced rapidly over the assembly.

"Here I am," she repeated, stepping forward. "Do you wish me?"

Sister Agatha hesitated; she did not know exactly what answer to make. How very unfortunate that Carmen should have been late on this particular day, thus rendering it impossible to prepare her beforehand for what might occur! Even now Sister Agatha would gladly have spoken with her alone, and told her gently about the choice which had fallen upon her. But Jonathan had already advanced to meet the girl. He had resumed his usual manner, and as he fixed his eyes on the unsuspecting maiden, there was a certain air of assured triumph in his looks, as if he had her now securely in his power.

"Dear Sister Carmen," he said, "you have, by your tardiness, missed hearing that Brother Daniel Becker has written to us from the land of the Caffres, and has desired us to choose a wife for him. The lots have just now been cast, and the Lord has directed it to you."

"To me?" said Carmen, with an air of perplexity, turning her astonished glance on the speaker, as if she did not understand what he was saying.

"Yes, to you, dear Sister," continued Jonathan, with a louder voice; "and I hope you will receive this choice humbly, as becomes you, and accept your position as Brother Daniel's wife -" he hesitated a moment, and then added with emphasis; "if you are not already betrothed to some other man."

Carmen's eyes flashed with anger, and she drew herself up proudly.

"Cast lots for me!" she exclaimed bitterly; "disposed of me at a chance, as if I were a bale of goods, a lifeless piece of machinery! Promised me to a man to whom no impulse of my heart draws me; to whom it is quite indifferent whether I or some other girl falls to his share - and all in the name of religion! This is indeed degradation, slavery! It never could be worse among the slaves on the islands whose freedom you all have taken so much trouble to secure."

She had spoken with all the passion of her warm nature stirred to its depths; and now she stopped, exhausted. All color had vanished from her face; only the lustrous eyes glistened with a dangerous light.

"I will never submit to your inspired decision, and refuse to recognize this choice," she said at length.

Every one looked at her in amazement, thunderstruck at this candid and straightforward announcement. All at once, as if she had been struck with leprosy, the Sisters shrank back from her - she stood alone in their midst; only Agatha approached her, and with an anxious look seized her hand.

"Dear Sister," she commenced gently, "you are excited, and cannot listen to the higher voice. Reflect a moment."

Carmen shook her head, and with that peculiar mixture of pride and child-like humility which marked her character, she bowed herself submissively before her faithful admonisher.

"Forgive me, dear Sister Agatha," she pleaded, embracing her fondly; "forgive me if I am constrained to speak in a manner that you think is wrong; but I can retract nothing of what I have said. Let me go to my father; he is my natural protector, and he alone has the right to dispose of me."

She avoided looking at Jonathan again; it seemed as if this new trouble must, in some way, have originated with him; and every pure, womanly instinct of her nature felt insulted. Gently unclasping her arms from Agatha's neck, she left the room. It was not possible to remain longer in the house; something impelled her to get out into the fresh air, by that means to throw off, if possible, some subtle influence which seemed to be weaving a spell over her.

As she hurried along, dark clouds began to scud across the sky overhead, and the low mutterings of thunder came from the distance. It may have been the thunderings of nature, or of war - she did not heed them; her heart was filled with bitter, rebellious thoughts, and her flying feet seemed to skim over the road; nor did she check her hasty steps until she was about to enter her father's room. Mauer sat in his arm-chair, absorbed in thought. She threw herself down on her knees beside him, and flung her arms about his waist. Pressing her head against his breast, she said half breathlessly: "Father, protect me!"

He looked at his daughter with a bewildered air. Only one hour ago so gay and light-hearted, and now so utterly unnerved, crouching in despair at his feet! Raising her up, he gazed into her pale countenance.

"Heavens above! what has befallen you, my child?"

"Father, they have cast lots for your child!"

"Cast lots?"

"Yes; cast lots, as for a thing that does not live and feel - a toy, that has no will of its own, no self-respect; given as a prize to a man who is nothing to me. And it is all done in the name of religion! Father, protect me!"

"Cast lots!" the old man repeated, as if his brain could not grasp what his ear heard. "No! Heaven forbid that such a misfortune, should befall you! It is enough that one of us has suffered and lived through such an ordeal. No, Carmen, be at rest, my darling. Your father will tell the elders that he cannot do without his child."

The faintest shadow of a smile appeared again on Carmen's lips as she listened to his comforting words, and she breathed more freely.

"I knew you would help me, my own dear father! I rejected the choice, and hastened to you for support."

"But for whom have they selected you as a wife?" asked Mauer, gently stroking her cheek.

"For Daniel Becker, the missionary who, six months ago, went to the land of the Caffres. Oh, father, you will not let me go from you? We will remain together; no one shall separate us - not even this Jonathan -" She involuntarily shuddered. At mention of that name the old man started and fixed his eyes on her.

"Jonathan?" he asked slowly. "Why do you blame him?"

"Father, I feared to speak of it," she stammered, shocked that she had so clearly betrayed herself. "He is your friend, and you become so agitated when he is mentioned. But you must listen now. Before your return he asked me, from Sister Agatha, for his wife; and after I refused him - for oh, father, I cannot help it, I have an aversion to him - he pursued me with a wild love that frightened me. He embraced and kissed me against my will, and then begged I would be silent about it. I promised; but that was before I knew I had a father living. Now I have told it, and I am glad you know all about the matter."

Her eyes rested trustingly on him, but she could not catch a responsive glance; he kept his head turned away, and looked out into the distance with a countenance full of distress and anguish.

"Dear father, are you angry with me?" she asked humbly.

"Not angry, no; but it is a misfortune - a great misfortune," he whispered.

At this moment there was a knock at the door; it opened, and Brother Jonathan entered. Father and daughter stared at him without stirring; no one uttered a word; no one moved. Mauer remained leaning back in his chair; Carmen did not rise from her kneeling posture, and only pressed her head closer to her father's bosom.

Jonathan silently regarded the pair. Never had Carmen looked more beautiful than in this clinging posture - in this outpouring of love and confidence. To see her thus reclining on her father's breast was nothing to give rise to jealous feelings, but it increased his longing to have her leaning thus on him.

"You are troubled; I know it, and have come to help you," he said at last, in his gentlest tones. "I am sorry, very sorry, that Sister Carmen has allowed herself to be so far carried away by her feelings as to lose all sense of duty and humility, and to speak such wild words before the people. We must see if things cannot be arranged pleasantly. I will consider what can be done, if Carmen will permit me to act at all for her in the matter."

"Dear Brother, spare me my child," pleaded Mauer, with faltering voice. "She cannot accept the lot which has fallen on her; she must not go so far from me just now, when I have found her again. I cannot live without my daughter."

"You know, dear Brother," returned Jonathan, "we of the faith always recognize in the casting of lots the most direct indication of the will of Heaven. Each one must fulfil the duty laid upon him, and not pause to consider if it concurs with his own wishes or not. If Carmen's hand is still free, she must follow the call which has been given her. She may not be separated from us forever. Perhaps in a few years she will return with her husband."

"A few years! Will they be granted to me?" said Mauer, sadly.

"Dear brother, I have already remarked that if Carmen is

M. CORVUS

already betrothed, the choice made by lot is null and void, and the elders must be requested to give their consent to the alliance she has in view," replied Jonathan, sharply, emphasizing each word.

Carmen's lip curled scornfully as he spoke, and the cutting, scathing glance she gave him was enough to wither a braver man than he. She surmised what he was aiming at, but uttered never a word. Leaning against her father's heart, she felt sure of finding there a secure resting-place, and a precious sense of sheltering love made her able to endure anything. But her proud glance roused Jonathan's spirit, which grew hotter and hotter under his calm exterior. Would he be compelled to give her up?

He could not satisfy himself whether his feeling for the girl was love or hate; at any rate, he thought within himself that to bend her pride and destroy her fancied security would afford him infinite satisfaction.

"But she is not betrothed," said Mauer, when Jonathan ceased speaking. "I, as her father, am the natural guardian of her destiny. I have the right to decide."

"The right, dear Brother?" interposed Jonathan, with a scornful smile. "That depends. It could not be granted to every parent in the Brotherhood." And as the old man before him dropped his eyes, he added smiling: "Yet if I asked, for the sake of old times, that you would give me Carmen for my wife, would I be able to gain your consent, as her father?"

It was a helpless, imploring look that Mauer now directed towards his daughter; his hands clasped over hers with a convulsive grasp; his lips moved, as if to speak, but no sound came from them.

Carmen looked at her father in perfect amazement.

"Father, dear father, indeed I cannot become the wife of this man," she whispered with a beseeching tone.

"Child, cannot you make yourself do it for my sake?" were the words wrung from his lips.

"No, never! Urge me not, my father; it would bring untold misery on me, and afford happiness to no one."

A deep flush rose to Jonathan's brow, and anger and disappointment completely triumphed over self-control. "You cannot be my wife, Sister Carmen? Very well; then you will be the wife of Brother Daniel in the land of the Caffres. Do you think I am going to tolerate your rebellious, stubborn spirit, which is so unsuitable to a member of our community? Let your father tell you that I have the means in my hands to compel you to decide between the two fates!"

As he spoke, Carmen sprang up, and, drawing herself to her full height, measured him with a proud, contemptuous look; then, as if unable to bring herself to address him, she turned to her father and said calmly: "Dear father, speak for your child, and protect her!"

She clasped her hands imploringly; while he shook his head in sorrow and grief, but remained silent.

"Father," she cried, "have you nothing to say?"

No sound issued from his pallid lips; the anguish of his soul was betrayed only in his eyes.

Burying her face in her hands, Carmen now broke down utterly; and Jonathan's evil countenance gleamed with triumph. As she appeared before him, bowed in despair and grief, like some beautiful flower crushed by a ruthless hand, his eyes feasted themselves on the lovely girl, who was at last humbled and forced to give herself to him.

"You will do well to consider the matter calmly, and give me your final decision, Brother Michael. I will return this evening for it. We will try to help each other in a spirit of brotherly love, and you well know I am willing to exercise mercy and patience, as we are commanded; but there are times when both must cease." Saying thus, he left the room.

*   *   *   *   *   *

Brother Mauer sat alone with his daughter, and a deathly silence enwrapped the two, left alone together with their grief. The sky was still dark, with threatening dark clouds, which threw their deep shadows over the room, and at intervals a blinding flash of lightning illuminated with dazzling ray the bowed figures of father and daughter; while loud claps of thunder called to them, as if to rouse them from the sorrowful trance.

But they stirred not. Outside, the rain poured in torrents, and the wind swept howling by; but they seemed not to hear. At last Mauer's hand felt its way to the girl's head, and passed lovingly and gently over it. She caught his fingers, as if the very touch inspired her with new life; and raising her head, she turned her hot, tearless eyes up to him, saying in an inexpressibly sad tone:

"Father, why have you forsaken your child in her hour of need?"

"Because, Carmen, I am powerless before this man," he returned in a low voice.

"Powerless?" she asked. "But how can he have any power over you if you do not wish it? He, a friend, against his friend!"

"Ah, Carmen," answered the old man, "that he has not used his power against me before is another proof of his friendship for me; but now, when he sees fit to exert it, I cannot prevent him, and must bear it. I have already told you that it is a great misfortune that he loves you, and you cannot return his affection."

"Father, my thoughts are so perplexed by all this. I cannot understand how any one can have such power over you that you are forced to leave your own child unprotected."

Mauer sighed deeply. Carmen rose, and began to pace restlessly up and down the room. Outside, the thunderstorm raged with ungovernable fury; within, the poor girl was endeavoring to quiet the tumult of her aching heart, and collect her scattered thoughts.

"Father," she said at last, breaking silence, and seating herself near him, "speak, and let me know how and why Brother Jonathan can injure you. What can we do to avert the peril we are in?"

"Carmen, could you bear to behold in your father a culprit, a great sinner?" He looked so crushed, so very, very miserable, that her loving heart overflowed with sympathy and pity. To look at that dear face, and see the wretchedness of gulf and remorse written there, wrung her heart beyond endurance, and brought the scalding tears to her eyes. She threw her arms about his neck, and answered tenderly: "You cannot be guilty in your daughter's eyes; and if you appear so before the world, I will only love you the more for it, and help you to bear your grief, father." He sobbed aloud, and drew her closer to him.

"It must be God's gracious mercy and pity which speaks to me through you, my child. May He bless you, and for your sake, and my sufferings, may He forgive my great sin! It is indeed an old story of guilt and sorrow which I have to tell, and which has weighed heavily upon my heart for nineteen long years! Listen, then, Carmen."

Mauer sat silent a moment, as if trying to refresh in his

memory the half-faded events of long years ago, and shape into more definite forms their outlines, obscured by the mists of time.

At length he spoke.

"Thirty years ago, my child, I left here with my first wife, and moved to Jamaica to carry on the linen business, for the Brothers had established themselves in business in connection with the mission there. We arrived in May, and were in a short time quite settled. The country and climate are lovely at that time of the year, but during the rainy season, when the wet ground sent forth its poisonous miasma, we both were stricken down with the fever. I, being the stronger, recovered from the attack pretty soon; but my wife, a small, delicate woman, succumbed at once to the fell destroyer.

"For two years I remained a widower, and led a lonely life of hard work. Gladly would I have returned home to Europe, but the business once begun was not so easily given up; it would have been attended with great losses. Therefore I wrote home, saying I needed a wife, and would like one sent out to me. I named two Sisters of whom I had thought, hoping that one or the other would come to me. One of them was dead, the other married; so the lot was cast among the other Sisters, and it fell on Sister Julie. When my new wife arrived, I was greatly shocked. She was, not only homely of face, but deformed in figure. In spite of my love for the beautiful, I conquered myself, and hoped she would be so much the more lovely in disposition. But hers was a narrow, severe nature, from which no congeniality could be expected. She prayed zealously and worked diligently carrying out with the greatest precision the rules prescribed for us; but she had not a single idea beyond that; and when she was not praying, was peevish, suspicious, and avaricious. For nearly eight years I lived with her, my aversion daily increasing. About that time, as misfortune would have it, a friend, who was living in Jamaica, died, owing me a large sum of money. His affairs were left in such confusion that I was obliged to receive the plantation as payment for my debt. I found the place in a wretched condition, and, in order to oversee its management to any advantage, I resolved to transfer my business in the mission to an agent, and move on the place with my wife. Then came a fatal hour for me. Into my darkened soul, into the comfortless, emptiness of my life, entered the power of a great passion.

"A slave belonging on a plantation about two hours' ride from mine, and owned by a Spaniard, ran away, and fled to me for protection. The slaves all knew that my laborers were free, and that induced the unhappy creature thither. Don Manuel was not a hard master, but the poor wretch had committed a grave fault, and was afraid to go home. So I resolved to ride over and speak with Don Manuel about it. I reached the hacienda of the Spaniard, and as I was about to enter, saw, reclining in a hammock under the palm-trees, a slight, delicate figure robed in white. Her arms were thrown above her head, and the lace of her sleeve falling back gave me a glimpse of the beautifully rounded limb. The sound of my horse's hoofs aroused her; she glided gracefully from the hammock, and looked at me with a curious expression of surprise as a quick blush mantled her cheek. She was scarcely more than a child, being only fifteen, but the loveliest, the most fascinating creature my eyes ever beheld. It was Inez - your mother.

"I was ushered into her father's presence, and while discussing business with him, watched her on the veranda feeding the peacocks and caressing a cunning little black monkey. I could not turn my eyes from her; each attitude seemed more exquisite than the last; each tone of her voice sounded like music.

"When I rode away, she was standing under the trees, and waved her hand to me in farewell. Turning after a moment, to see if she was still there, I beheld the same lovely picture, which lives in my heart to this day."

Mauer paused, affected by his own words. Before his mind's eye rose the past in all its beauty; and a crowd of sweet memories overwhelmed him. Carmen had listened with intense eagerness to his recollections of her mother; she had almost forgotten that she was about to hear the confession of a great crime. With a smile parting her lips, she looked at her father, impatient for him to proceed.

"How this storm rages!" Mauer resumed; "and yet it is nothing compared with the blows they have in the West Indies. Can you remember them, Carmen? One September, a few weeks after my visit to Don Manuel, the sea-breeze lulled, and we were almost suffocated with the heat. For many days the heavens were overcast with leaden clouds, which grew darker and darker as they continued to pile up in huge masses; electric flashes danced and quivered through them, and a continual rumbling of thunder threatened danger, and indicated that the rainy season was approaching. I had been to the mission to look after my business, and was riding slowly homeward, through the heavy sultry air, when all at once the storm broke over me. It came tearing down from the blue mountains, raging and driving over the savannas in unchecked fury. I put spurs to my horse, in a fruitless effort to reach home before the worst came, for I knew full well what would follow this outbreak. At this moment I saw approaching me, at full speed, a white horse, whose rider was making hopeless attempts to manage him. I at once recognized Inez, and placing myself across the path, succeeded in seizing the bridle and stopping the animal in his mad night.

"No time was now to be lost in bringing the girl home to her father, and in such a storm my presence was necessary for her protection. She had been riding alone, as usual, and on the return home her horse had taken the wrong road. The storm became more and more violent; the lightning nearly blinded us, and terrified our horses. The rain now began to pour down in torrents, and it was impossible for Inez to retain her seat in the saddle. She remembered a little deserted negro cabin in the neighborhood, under a grove of magnolias, and thither we fled. There was no light in the hut; the wind bent the trees down on its roof and dashed the rain against its sides, so that we expected every moment to be killed. Inez drew closer to me and trembled violently, as I supported her quivering form with my arm. I spoke soothingly to her, as I would have done to a timid child; and as I bent over to comfort her, a flash of lightning lit up the place, so that I could look into her eyes dilated with fear, and she into mine. Then - she kissed me again and again. Carmen, your mother was one of the most innocent, the purest beings on earth; in her heart was no impure thought, in her life was no action which could not bear the light of day. But there, under the glowing, tropical skies, blood flies quicker through the veins than here in our cool Germany; and from childhood to womanhood is but one, sudden leap. When I felt her kisses on my lips, I was taken aback; I had thought of her only as a beautiful child, but now I recognized the woman in her, and - I was a married man.

"A sound of anxious hallooing reached our ears. It was made by the negroes which Don Manuel had sent out in search of his child; and as the first fury of the storm had now spent itself, we parted from each other.

"When I reached home, my unfortunate wife seemed more repulsive than ever; in fact, her disagreeable ways, added to her natural homeliness, had rendered her almost intolerable. The memory of Inez's lovely form and face, her graceful manner and silvery voice, was ever present with me. I repeatedly told myself how wicked this was, and resolved not to call again on Don Manuel, lest I should see her. But it was impossible to banish her image, and day after day the struggle within my soul grew more severe. Thus the rainy months passed away; during which I scarcely left home at all, and saw no one but my wife. One day she was taken sick, and soon became so ill that Brother Jonathan, who was the physician of the mission, and for whom I sent at once, became very anxious. It was on the fifth day of her illness, and Jonathan had been to see her in the afternoon; but in the evening she became much worse. She complained so much that about ten o'clock I concluded to ride out to the doctor's. Jonathan was much sought after as a physician, and when I reached his house about eleven o'clock, he had already been roused up from his sleep by a man who wanted some medicine for a child, and who was waiting to have it prepared. Ah, how I remember every trifle, exactly as if it all had occurred only yesterday!

"When I told Jonathan how very ill my wife was, he gave me very little if any hope, but said he would prepare a soothing draught for her. I was full of anxiety and in great haste to get back, as was also the other man; and when at last Thomas, Jonathan's servant, brought the two bottles of medicine, I seized mine eagerly, as I had a long way to go; and as I left, Brother Jonathan said to me: 'They are opium-drops; give her fifteen when you get home, and if she does not get easy, then two hours after repeat the dose.'"

"I sprang on my horse and hurried away. Jonathan's words seemed to ring in my ears: 'I have scarcely any hope of saving her.' Ah, Carmen, they were to me like words of deliverance. I had borne for so long the fearfully heavy yoke which had been laid upon me that at times it seemed beyond human endurance; for this woman's soul was almost more repulsive than her body. At last I reached home. It was twelve o'clock. My wife was suffering as much as ever; she complained incessantly of the increasing pain, and I at once prepared the drops for her. She groaned; then I began to count the drops: one, two, three, four - and then the thought came into my mind: 'Scarcely any more hope.' My hand trembled; a mist seemed to gather before my eyes. The drops fell, faster; I counted on: thirteen, fourteen, fifteen; a few drops more had fallen unawares into the spoon; then followed one more, and again one more - twenty-five, twenty-six. I pushed the vial away from me. 'Where are the drops? Give them to me!' she cried with sinking voice. She snatched the spoon from my hand, and I turned away my head. My good angel had forsaken me."

Mauer groaned and hid his face in his hands. Carmen held her breath; she dared not speak, or raise her eyes to look at her father; she could not even think.

"The patient," resumed Mauer, after a short pause, "became quieter; her breathing was scarcely audible. Did she sleep? From my heart I prayed: 'God of mercy, let her sleep and not die - not now!' But I did not dare to look at or listen to her. I threw myself on a couch, and, in the horror that filled my soul, buried my head in the cushions. Time passed on; the clock ticked as usual, I know not whether for minutes or hours. Then I heard the ring of horse's hoofs before the door. I got up to let the visitor in, for the servants were in bed. It was only three o'clock in the morning. To my surprise, in walked Brother Jonathan. 'How is she?' he inquired hastily; and I answered softly, 'She sleeps.'

"He approached the side of the bed, and drawing the lamp near, so as to observe her closely, said: 'Yes, never to wake again. I was sure nothing could save her!'

"I did not utter a word; my tongue seemed glued to my mouth, and refused to move. Had she died because nothing could save her, or because I had dropped double the number of drops? The fatal vial still stood on the table by the bed where I had placed it. I feared to touch it again; but Jonathan took it up, and, looking at it, said casually: 'Did you give her from it twice? I see there are more than fifteen drops gone.' I nodded my head. 'After two hours?' he asked again, and put the vial in his pocket. I again nodded affirmatively. He examined the dead woman again, felt her skin, and raised her eyelids. 'Strange,' he said. 'You gave her the first dose about twelve o'clock, and the second at two; it is now only three o'clock, and this corpse has been cold for several hours. Your wife must have died at least two hours ago; how is that?' He looked at me in perplexity, and I felt myself grow pale under his inquiring glance; my limbs refused to support me, and I sank fainting on the floor.

"The funeral was over; I had suffered with another attack of fever, and was restored to my usual health, when one day a hasty messenger summoned me to go at once to Don Manuel, who needed my presence. He had been thrown from his horse, and was suffering intensely from internal injuries, which threatened to terminate fatally at any moment. I was conducted to his bedside, at which Inez knelt, her face buried on her father's pillow. At the foot of the bed stood the physician, Brother Jonathan.

"Don Manuel motioned me to his side. 'Don Mauer,' he said in a faint voice, 'I must die; but, before I leave this world, I would like to provide for the future of my child, who, as you know, has no mother. You have saved her life in the storm, and she has confessed to me that she loves you, and hopes you return her affection. Therefore I ask you now, while death is hastening on, can you love her? And will you take her to your heart, to love and cherish her as your wife? She has always been a good daughter to me; she will be a true and faithful wife to you.'

"Inez raised her lovely head, and her dark eyes, which, in their innocence did not know how to veil her sentiments, looked pleadingly at me. I laid one hand on the graceful, girlish head, and the other in that of the dying man.

"'I will vow to honor and cherish her as my most precious treasure,' I said solemnly, 'for I love her above everything on earth.'

"Inez sank into my arms, and the weak voice of her dying

father pronounced a blessing on us. He begged that a priest might be quickly brought, to unite us by his death-bed, so that he would know Inez was safely provided for.

"Scarcely was the ceremony over, when he drew his last breath.

"The surprise, the overwhelming emotion, caused by this event, impressed me so powerfully that I could think of nothing but the one fact - 'Inez is mine!' When I left the house, after handing the weeping girl over into the hands of her faithful nurse. Brother Jonathan rode along with me.

"'Brother Michael,' he said, glaring at me darkly and menacingly, 'I now know what sinful love prompted you to give Julie, your wife, a double dose of opium; and why, when I came to see her early in the morning, the corpse had already been cold for some hours.'

"As I felt myself turn pale, and answered nothing, he laughed scornfully, turned his horse's head, and rode off in another direction. After that the sight of Brother Jonathan became torture to me. I always read the terrible accusation in his face, although he has never uttered it; and I soon found he was equally obnoxious to my wife. Indeed, she actually hated him; for, as she told me, he had persecuted her with his love, long before I had ever been to Don Manuel's. She shunned him as much as possible, whenever he came to the hacienda; and it was most welcome news to both her and me when he told us his health could not stand the climate any longer, and he only needed money to take him to a colder climate. I gave him several thousands out of my fortune, so as to get rid of him; and he, with his negro servant Thomas, went to Bethlehem in Pennsylvania. To my relief, I saw no more of him; he wrote to me some time afterwards, but I did not answer, and never heard from him again. All this time the worm of self-accusation was gnawing at my heart; but as long as Inez lived, I found happiness in her love, so that not even the voice of conscience could be heard. But when she was taken from me, then the cry arose in my heart: 'This is my punishment; she has died for my sin!' and all peace vanished from my existence. It was then that I formed the resolution to atone with my life for the crime. I longed to sacrifice myself; to suffer for the Lord's sake, and win over souls to the truth. I parted from you, the one single thing that remained to me of Inez. I sold my lands in Jamaica, and went wherever I was ordered - across the seas to India, where the least work had as yet been done, and to various other parts of the world. The rest you already know. No one can imagine how gladly I have suffered, although those years of slavery and misery were very grievous. I hoped thereby to win the favor of Heaven; and when I was at last permitted to return home, I thought I saw in that an assurance that my crime was forgiven. But it is all a mistake, Carmen, for Brother Jonathan lives, and is here, and he is a perpetual reproach to me. Every word he utters seems to refer to it, and I never fail to shrink with pain from having him touch the sore point. He has it in his power to bring my sin to light, at any time; and it is an evidence of his great friendship for me that he has been hitherto silent. If either you or I anger him, he will not allow our old friendship to influence him any longer. You have heard his threat, and he will, without fail, carry it out. I will bear submissively whatever comes; but I am not able, my dear child, to protect you. If you refuse him for your husband, he will disclose my guilt, and I, a criminal, can do nothing for you, but must quietly bow before the inevitable."

He was silent, and dared not look at Carmen, for he feared to read what might be written on her countenance. She sat perfectly still, absorbed in her own thoughts, her hand shading her eyes, and her breath heaving quickly. The blood seemed frozen with horror in her veins at what she had heard; her brave heart quailed before the dreadful future, which she knew not how to meet. And yet one thought stood prominently forth from the rest: she must prove her love for her father at any cost. He needed it sorely now, and she had only a short hour ago declared she would love him the better for his fault, and thus help him to bear his misery. He had sinned for the sake of her mother, who surely would have forgiven him and loved him, whatever other people might have felt. The daughter, must not set herself up to condemn her father. God would judge him mercifully, according to the depth of his repentance and suffering. Of this she felt perfectly assured; so, raising her head and turning her face to her father, she threw her arms about the old man's neck.

"Be comforted, dear father, and trust in God!" she said lovingly. "You have atoned so deeply and long that your sin is surely forgiven, and I am sure we will find some way out of this dreadful trouble."

She was silent a moment, sunk in deep thought. "I must inherit my dear mother's aversion to Brother Jonathan, for I have felt it as long as I can remember, and it would be quite impossible to give myself to him. I hate him as I do the Evil One. I could believe anything, however bad, about him; and yet what he does is good, always good, and he has shown himself a friend to you. Let us consider if there may not be some way out of this dreadful dilemma."

The old man leaned, sobbing, against the girl whom he, as a father, should have been able to succor, and whose poor brains were now racked with caring for both herself and him.

*   *   *   *   *   *

The fury of the storm had spent itself, but the rain still poured in torrents, when, towards five o'clock in the afternoon, two companies of soldiers, which had been manoeuvring during the day, came marching along, in rather disorderly fashion, on the highroad to the settlement.

"It is well the order to bivouac in this deluge has been

M. CORVUS

countermanded, for we would certainly have been drowned like rats," said one of the two officers, who were marching a little in advance. "Yet almost anything would have been preferable to taking up our quarters with these pious people, whom I doubt will give us any sort of a welcome. They look on us as cannibals and murderers, and I tremble to think how their untiring zeal will urge them on to attempt our conversion."

His companion laughed. "It will not be so bad as you think, Hansen; although I must admit I don't think our wild boys will be very welcome guests to them. It will sadly disturb their extreme orderliness and quiet routine of life."

"You are sure of being well received, Captain Trautenau," resumed the first speaker, "having already been in this Bethany, and also having a sister at school here among the saints. You must look out for us, and get the best shelter you can."

Having now reached the suburbs of the village, Alexander von Trautenau ordered a halt to be made and the soldiers fall in rank. "We will march in with as imposing an appearance as possible," he said gayly; and they passed through the streets, while many a terrified and astonished form rushed to the windows and watched them go by. Alexander, being familiar with the place, marched with his men directly to the Brothers' house and entered the spacious yard; there he gave the command to stack arms. That surely was a peaceful proceeding! The Brothers' house was much larger than that of the Sisters, as here they usually carried on their various branches of industry. The door was now opened and, with a pale, terror-stricken countenance, Brother Martin, the presiding elder, stepped out. Alexander immediately went up to him, and asked politely: "Are you the elder in authority over this house?" When he answered in the affirmative, Alexander continued: "I have been ordered here with two companies to find shelter for the night, as the heavy rain has rendered bivouacking impossible. Will you be so good as to assign me quarters for the men?"

"We will, mein Herr. But, first of all, tell me, I pray, if these guns are loaded," answered Brother Martin, pointing anxiously to the stacks of arms.

"Of course the guns are loaded, but only with powder; and there is no danger whatever of their going off by themselves," said the officer, trying to reassure him.

But Brother Martin only grew paler than before. "Herr Officer, I must humbly beg that the guns be removed."

"With pleasure," replied Alexander, "if you will show me a room in which my men may carry them and keep them dry."

Brother Martin hastened with alacrity into the house, and opened a room in the basement. The murderous weapons were carried in by the soldiers, the door was shut, and, to the great relief of the poor elder, the key turned and put away safely in the officer's pocket.

Meanwhile, Hansen had not been able to repress his ridiculing remarks. "It is enough to turn an honest soldier's heart around in his body to listen to such stuff," he said. "Guns! As if we would carry anything else! The man must be a fool."

Alexander divided his men into squads, to occupy the apartments where they were to be accommodated with pallets of straw.

One of the married brothers now came up and addressed the captain. "Herr Officer," he said modestly, "I have room in my house for a few men. Will you allow me to accommodate four or six? I promise to give them the very best that my poor house affords."

"With many thanks, kind sir," was the reply. "Please select from among them those you would like to have; the poor drenched creatures will be only too glad of your hospitality."

The man chose the first six which came to hand, and carried them off with him. The ice being thus broken, one brother after another offered to take in some of them, and pretty soon everything was satisfactorily arranged. Another Brother begged to have the officers for his guests, and with hearty hospitality withdrew to prepare the best of everything the simple larder afforded for the entertainment of the strangers.

Clean white linen was spread over the table and refreshments of every kind were brought out. Pretty soon the provision-wagon arrived. Meat and vegetables were unpacked, and preparations were made to prepare the evening meal. The pioneers commenced to take up the paving-stones in the yard, in order to make a deep hollow in which to light the fire; but Brother Martin rushed out perfectly horrified.

"Herr Captain, you surely will not allow your good people to kindle a fire here in the yard? I beg that you will forbid it; there is no knowing what mischief might result from it; and besides, it will ruin the yard."

"But where, then, can the men cook their supper if it is too dangerous here?" asked Alexander, somewhat impatiently. "The men are wet and hungry, and have had no regular meal to-day; they must be permitted to prepare something warm to eat."

"Oh, of course," said Martin, with compassion. "We will not let them suffer, and I will gladly allow you the use of a large kitchen, where all the cooking for the Brothers is done every day."

The proposition was received with many thanks. Every convenience which the house afforded was offered for the comfort of the men.

"Trautenau," said Hansen, rubbing his hands with satisfaction, "things seem very good about here; and if they don't try to convert us, in addition, it will be the best place we have found quarters in for a long time. The sneaks have even a glass of choice wine in their cellar, and we will forgive Brother Martin's horror of our weapons in hopes that he will give us a taste of it. I thought they drank only water, and would be very much scandalized to hear of wine being anywhere about their premises."

"Hush your mocking, Hansen, else I will not answer for your being allowed to remain in this paradise. I hope you will not disgrace me while I go to seek my sister, before it is too late. You know we march early in the morning."

* * * * * *

Carmen and her father had been too deeply absorbed in their sorrows to observe what was transpiring in the settlement. The outer world had vanished completely from their minds. Concluding finally to leave everything undecided until after the interview between the old man and Jonathan, Carmen turned her steps homeward, for it was after eight o'clock. After ascending the steps, she remained standing under the arched portico in front of the house, trying to forget herself, her father, everything. She felt as if her own conscience was in some way guilty; and then, too, what was to become of her now? His crime, and her duty as a daughter, urged her imperatively into the arms of this man whom she thoroughly despised. There seemed no way of escape. The idea flashed across her brain to renounce her identity with the Moravians; but that would be synonymous with total separation from her father, for in his present frame of mind, when he was continually dwelling on repentance and reparation, he would never tear himself away from his old faith. Leave her father? Never! One thought tempted her - the thought of Wollmershain and Frau von Trautenau; but she put it resolutely from her: she could not, she dared not; she had no claim on any one there, and here she belonged to her father.

Ah, how her poor bleeding heart ached! If she could only weep, perhaps it would help to lighten the weary burden which was crushing her to the earth; but no relieving tears would come to her burning eyes. At last she sat down on a ledge of the wall near the doorway, to rest in solitude a little while, and to try to compose herself before going into the house. It had now ceased raining, and a dimly-burning lantern which was hung near by dispelled the darkness in a measure, and threw its uncertain rays over the wet stones of the yard, and over Carmen's drooping figure. The streets were perfectly quiet, the water dripped monotonously from the roofs, now and then the footsteps of some solitary passer-by echoed faintly on the ear, followed by the deep silence, broken only by the falling drops. There was something soothing in this great hush of nature; and the gentle dripping seemed like a loving voice singing some tired child to sleep; Carmen felt as if drawn within a magic circle. For a long time she sat there, till at last she heard a step approaching from the distance, and a man made his appearance in the light of the lantern. Something sparkled and glittered on his coat; and as he strode along with quick, firm steps, the spurs on his boots clanked. Carmen saw and heard it all as if in her sleep. Still motionless, she sat staring out into the darkness, and her heart, her poor heart, seemed dead and cold. There! did not the stranger enter the portico? He certainly did; and, as his figure became more distinctly discernible in the uncertain light, her pulses began to throb violently - those pulses which she a moment ago believed would never again beat with lively emotion. She leaned back closer to the wall, and stared at the figure with wide-opened eyes. As the man ascended the steps and saw the shrinking form close against the wall, he started, hesitated a moment, and then, putting his hand to his cap in greeting, said joyfully: "Fraulein Carmen, can it really be you? I have come, although it is so late, to greet you, and make the acquaintance of your father, as I am here only for to-night, and leave early in the morning. Adele told me I would find you here, in the house with the portico." He spoke with a glad tone and put out his hand, for at Wollmershain they had parted with a hearty hand-shake, and now he ventured on the same privilege.

The girl laid her hand in his; it was so cold and clammy it chilled him; and Carmen, as she leaned her head back against the stone wall, had such a tired, weary, wretched look that he could not refrain from asking with an anxious air: "For Heaven's sake! Surely some misfortune has happened to you! Carmen, dear Fraulein Carmen, I implore you, tell me just one word, that I may know what is the matter, and help you if I can."

She had risen slowly and with difficulty, for her knees trembled, and she could scarcely stand. He kept her hand in his as if to assist her, and pressed it with gentle warmth. At the sound of his sympathizing voice, the heavy pressure on her tortured heart suddenly gave way, and agonized sobs burst from her lips, while a flood of scalding tears flowed from her eyes. Her slender frame shook with the violence of her emotion; and as he sought to support her with his arm, her head sank on his shoulder.

"Dear Carmen," he pleaded, "do not keep back from me the cause of this distress! You cannot know how I am racked with grief for you. What shall I say to convince you of my feelings? It troubles me sorely, oh, believe me, to find you in such sorrow."

His words seemed to increase the intensity of her grief; and yet how those blinding tears relieved her! What an angel of light he seemed - he, of whom she had once thought so differently! She did not repulse him now when his arm encircled her; but leaning on him confidingly, she somehow felt that he who held her was a true man; that he alone was able to help and comfort her, and that it was a precious privilege to have him near in this hour of need. She could not turn to her father for succor; that one great hope had melted away; but in this man she knew there was courage, as well as will and the power to assist her in her woe. As he poured question after question upon her, she attempted at last to speak.

"They have cast lots for me to-day," she stammered. "I am forced to be the wife of a man I despise - by lot, Herr Trautenau!"

"By lot?" he asked, flushing angrily. "You, our beautiful, proud Carmen, given away by lot? That is incredible! Your father will surely not permit it!"

"My poor father!" she cried. "He can take no step to prevent it; he cannot save me."

"But! - by heavens, I will not allow such a horrible thing!" he cried passionately, and drew her closer to him. "Carmen, I conjure you, I beseech you, not to submit to this shameful custom of your people!"

"No; I would rather die than do it!" she replied, as something of her old courage returned to her. Now that he stood by her, she felt that some escape might be possible. She dried her tears, and raised her pretty head, which had rested so wearily on his shoulder, endeavoring to free herself from a position which, now that she was calm enough to think, had become embarrassing to her. As she did so, she gave a terrified start, for, unheard by either of them, Brother Jonathan with his cat-like step had drawn near, and she now caught a glimpse of his hated countenance, distorted with scorn and anger.

"Rather die than be my wife?" he asked mockingly, as he approached nearer. "A pleasant answer, surely, for me to listen to! This is, then, the modest, prudish Sister whom I must not presume to touch! She refuses me, an honest man who loves her, and declines to follow the rules of her faith, only to throw herself into the arms of a strange interloper! Do you think we will have a Sister among us who bids defiance to all the meek love and submission, the decorum and modesty which is necessary for a member of our community? I, as superintendent of the Sisters, will now suggest to the Sister in charge that Carmen Mauer be expelled from our communion."

Carmen seemed not to hear these severe words. She breathed heavily, but answered not a word, only pressed her hands against her throbbing heart and raised her pale face to him calmly and indifferently, not seeming to care for his condemnation and threats.

"Fraulein Carmen," said Alexander, as Jonathan ceased speaking. His voice chased all fear from her heart, and she turned her gaze, full of trust and confidence, on him again.

"Fraulein Carmen," he continued, "you once told me that only your father's or your husband's arm should enfold you. When my arm supported you just now, you suffered it to do so; was it because you trusted my honor and love sufficiently to give me the right to protect you through all time as your husband?"

She gave him a quick glance of glad surprise.

"Yes," she replied with a firm voice, offering him her hand. He pressed it with passionate warmth.

"Mein Herr," he said coldly, turning to Jonathan, "will you have the kindness, as superintendent of the Sisters, to inform them that Fraulein Carmen Mauer and her betrothed husband, Captain von Trautenau, have gone to her father's apartments; that this lady, on account of her betrothal to me, declines the destiny chosen for her by lot;

and will, moreover, be obliged to leave the community and follow her husband? This may perhaps prevent any unpleasant misunderstanding." He bowed stiffly to the astounded Jonathan, drew Carmen's hand through his arm, and turned away.

Carmen had listened to his words in such a confused state of mind that she was powerless to resist even had she wished to. What he had said almost took away her breath; but as the strength of his arm, so that of his will, held her captive, and she would have followed him blindly to the end of the world. But now, when she was about to return to her father, she was torn with anguish for the poor sufferer who tarried alone in his room. He must be cared for at once; so, pausing a moment, she turned towards Jonathan. The threat he had hurled at her showed the point where she might gain the victory over him, and render him powerless to harm her father.

"Brother Jonathan," she said, "you told me that if I was affianced to some other man, the validity of the lot would be annulled. You now see that the threat against me is vain, but I would like to relate a little occurrence to the Brothers and Sisters which would not tend to increase the holy reputation which the pious Brother Jonathan Fricke now enjoys. You have been kind to my father up to this time; I beg that you will continue to be so in future, for your own sake. I would not willingly inflict any injury upon you; but the slightest hint from him will compel me - I think you understand."

Jonathan stood as if turned to stone as Alexander led Carmen away, saying:

"Let us go to your father."

When they reached the house, he opened the door and passed in with her.

"Wait a moment," he said, as they stood in the hall. "I was too hasty; the intense desire to save you dictated my impulsive question, and your prompt answer was called forth by the rashness of a man who, in all the heat of his fervent love, sought to avert an impending danger. But you shall not be compelled thus to resign your freedom. Tell me now calmly if you can love me a little; if otherwise, take back your hastily-given word, and after a while, when you can do so with perfect safety to yourself, let the world know that our engagement has ceased. Let my love shield you as long as it can; but only if you love me do I want you to marry me."

They had been talking in the dark; but now a faint light shone through the window and flickered on the girl's little white cap. It seemed like a halo to Alexander; he gazed at it fixedly, as if it were an omen of happiness for him.

Carmen had been standing with folded hands; now she raised her arms and clasped them gently about his neck. "I love you with my whole heart," she whispered softly, "and my happiness rests with you alone."

He drew her to his heart with a violent outbreak of passionate love; and it was almost as if with a sob that the strong man cried, "Carmen, my love, my darling!" and kissed her with all his heart on his lips.

CHAPTER X.

A faint sound of martial music penetrated to Brother Mauer's room the next morning, as the troops marched away. The old man sat wrapped in meditation. A new world of thought had opened to him since last night. Carmen, the bride of a stranger! How very different from any former plans or prospects! He had given his free consent to his daughter's marriage, for Alexander had gained his entire confidence.

The resolution and determined will displayed in the young officer's bearing reassured him, and dispelled his inward despair and helplessness. A marriage with this man was the only solution to the miserable situation; and when Carmen was removed from his immediate neighborhood, she would still be nearer than if she was a missionary's wife. But the severance of his child from her faith gave him extreme anxiety for her; as, according to his ideas, happiness, prosperity, and peace could be found only among the Moravians, in the strict observance of their laws and customs. Was it possible Carmen could be willing to forsake all this for a strange man? He could not grasp the thought. Yet when, weeping bitterly, she said, "Father, I love Alexander as deeply as my mother did you," there thrilled through him a memory of Inez's ardent love, as she clung to him with utter abandon, and found her world at his side; and he blessed the union of the lovers.

But Carmen had a very trying interview with Sister Agatha, when she went in the morning and imparted to her what had occurred the night before, and what decision she had made.

Agatha listened to the girl's words attentively and thoughtfully, and an expression of deep sorrow filled her countenance.

"Carmen," she said sadly, "judging from what you say, you have in your heart completely cut yourself off from the Lord's mercy and our faith, and therefore it is better that things should be as they are, for you must not play the hypocrite - anything is preferable to that. You would destroy yourself and be of no benefit to us." She laid her hand gently on Carmen's head, and added: "Go now, dear Sister, and tread the new path you have chosen for yourself; and Heaven grant it may not lead to misery! If, however, happiness deserts you, and your heart yearns after us, like the thirsty wayfarer in the desert, then return to the people of the Lord, that we may help you to return to Him."

She tenderly kissed the maiden's brow, pressed her to her bosom again and again, and let her go. She followed Carmen's lovely form with her eyes as she passed through the doorway and left the room; then, folding her hands in prayer, she said: "Lord, forgive the child. A soul which was entrusted to me by Thee, which I knew not how to guide aright, has been taken from me. If she goes astray, let mine be the blame, for it was my fault; but if she seeks Thee in another path of life, then give her Thy peace. Ah, how much I have still to correct in myself! Yet I would fain do my utmost for the souls Thou hast committed to my charge. I praise Thee, and would not think of my trials, if only I am counted worthy to suffer for Thy sake."

So Carmen was freed from the fetters she had unwillingly worn for so long. Alexander had arranged with her and her father that she should go to his mother at Wollmershain; but the separation from her father was a severe trial to her loving heart. Fate had scarcely united them, and already they must part and, knowing what misery it was to the old man, it seemed almost more than she could bear. And yet it must be. She promised to visit her father twice every week, and would be quick and diligent in her home duties, so as to make her visits longer.

The days were now very lonely without the bright, cheerful presence of his daughter; and when winter came, his own dwelling was ready to be occupied, but all the zest and pleasure of moving into his new abode seemed to have vanished. He took Sister Ursula, an aged widow, as his servant and housekeeper. How he loved to sit by the window in his room, from whence he could look out on the hill where the cemetery was laid out! "The Brothers will soon carry me along that path," he thought, "and it will be well for me when the time comes. I have always longed to be laid away in our own God's-acre, among the Sisters and Brothers, and enter with them into the joy of our Lord."

He now had also the happiness of having Carmen with him for several days at a time. The house seemed illuminated by her presence, her room was close to his, and there she had plants which he took care of for her. There was also a snug little corner where they passed many happy hours together. But with the knowledge of the fearful secret which over-shadowed her father's life a deeper gravity had come to her, which subdued her otherwise exuberant and joyous temperament; and Alexander often asked if it was the love she felt for him which had thus checked her former cheerfulness. And this shadow did not pass away when, shortly after Christmas, her wedding was celebrated, and Mauer informed her that he had divided the fortune left him by Inez from his own property, in order to make it over to her daughter, to whom it by right belonged. So the young couple remained at Wollmershain, after Alexander had sold his commission and left the army; and Mauer was happy in the assurance that his daughter would always be near him.

CHAPTER XI.

On a bleak November day, when all nature wore its most dreary aspect, the carriage of Herr von Trautenau, now well known in the village, drew up before Brother Mauer's door. The horses had scarcely stopped, when the door opened and Alexander sprang out, followed by Carmen, whose face bore traces of recent tears.

"Be brave, dear heart!" he said.

"I have you and our darling boy left," she answered with emotion; and turning back to the carriage, took a little child from the nurse's arms. She kissed him fondly, and the little fellow clapped his hands and crowed merrily at his mother as she held him in her arms. Then from beneath the flaxen ringlets which covered the infantile head a pair of large black eyes looked around with wonder at the strange place and the dark figure, with the white cap, that stood in the doorway.

Carmen was surprised to see Sister Agatha.

"Have I come too late?" she asked in a tone of anguish.

"No, dear Carmen, he still lives," said the faithful nurse, soothingly. "But he is failing rapidly since the attack this morning. He has been so weak of late that we have felt prepared for the end to come at any time. He has been asking anxiously for you since consciousness has returned, and Sister Ursula sent at once for me, that I might be with him while she went for another doctor, as Brother Jonathan has just been summoned to the country to visit the miller."

"How good you are, dear Sister Agatha!" said Carmen, pressing her hand affectionately.

They had now entered the house, and Alexander remained in an adjoining room, while Carmen went at once to her father. The bed had been drawn close to the window to give him more air, and he was now resting quietly, as if asleep, his hands crossed on his breast, and the shadow of death on his brow. Carmen was greatly shocked at the change.

"My darling father, I am here with you; do you know me, your own Carmen?" she asked, kneeling by the couch.

At the sound of her voice, he opened his eyes, and a faint, happy smile broke over his stiffening features.

"My child - are you here? Now I am ready to go."

"Father, let us hope God will spare you to us!"

"No, my precious child, let us hope He will, at last, set me free; for I long, oh so earnestly! to be at rest. Carmen, a guilty conscience is a scorpion which never ceases to torment, and deals a death-blow to all peace and happiness; therefore keep your heart pure, my darling, and ever have God's commandments before your mind, so as to avoid sinning against them. Let me persuade you to come back into the bosom of our faith, and draw your husband with you. He could enter the Brotherhood, even though he lived elsewhere. Oh, ensure the safety of your soul, under the shelter of our holy religion, so that your life be not poisoned with remorse, as mine has been!"

She kissed her father's hand with love and reverence; then raising her head, looked in his eyes, which rested on her so anxiously. "Father I promise you I will remain faithful to my God, and endeavor to keep His laws."

Mauer sank back on his pillows. "Brother Jonathan," he whispered, after a pause, "has kept my fearful secret; and even though he always involuntarily reminds me of it, he has maintained his friendship and brotherly love for me until now; but he has never allowed me to forget that my wealth must go to the community, as an atonement for my crime; so I have specified in my will that, in expiation of a great sin, I have left all my money to the commonwealth of the Brotherhood and their missions: thus, in benefiting all, to make amends for sinning against one."

Carmen silently kissed his pale lips; then, rising, went into the next room and brought back with her Alexander and the child. They kneeled beside the dying man, and Carmen asked with tears "Father, bless your children!"

"Do you value the blessing of such as I?" he said humbly.

"Yes, my father, I cannot live without it."

Then the old man laid his hands on the three heads and murmured words of benediction.

CHAPTER XII.

It was four o'clock in the afternoon, and the shadows of twilight began to gather on the gloomy sky. Agatha brought in a lamp, and all retired save Carmen; thus leaving her and her father alone together, undisturbed. Mauer lay quiet, with his eyes half closed; while his daughter sat holding his hand in a loving clasp, her head buried in the coverlid. In the stillness which prevailed in the chamber of death, the door was heard to open, and some one entered noiselessly; but the draught caused by the open window closed the door sharply behind the visitor. Mauer opened his eyes at the sound, and looked up vacantly as if he did not recognize Jonathan. Carmen also raised her head; but when she saw who it was, she immediately hid her face again, for she felt it quite impossible to speak to him now. Kneeling between the bed and the wall, her form was completely hidden in the dark shadow.

"Brother Mauer, I have just returned from the Country, and hear that you have been ill. What is the matter?" asked Jonathan.

At the sound of his voice, the sick man shivered as if from an icy breath of wind. He stared at the physician with dilated eyes.

"Brother Jonathan," he faltered, "the end has come, and the old, dark story will be laid with me in the grave. I know I have sinned grievously, but have atoned with a life of repentance and cruel suffering for the murder of an inoffensive wife."

As the old man spoke, Jonathan looked at him sharply and searchingly. The light of the lamp shone on his altered features, which bore the stamp of death. The physician seized his hand; the pulse was almost gone; there was no possibility of saving his life; each moment brought the end nearer. Then Jonathan's hate, revenge, and scorn broke loose, and flashed unrestrained from his eyes, which were fixed on the figure lying before him. For twenty years he had hated this man more than any other on earth; and for twenty years he had been obliged to put on the hypocrisy of love towards him. What a trial for his hot, seething passion! At the last, the moment had now come when his enemy was in his power, and he could throw up his visor and show his real face! Now was the time to crown his revenge, before the object of it passed entirely out of his reach forever.

Jonathan glanced hastily around the quiet darkened chamber, to convince himself that they were alone. He saw no one; the faint light showed only the pale features of the dying one pressed against the pillow. It was not possible that any one could be there! Old Ursula, the only other occupant of the house, had retired to the kitchen to weep and lament; and having passed directly up from the front door to the sick-room, he was ignorant of the presence of others in the dwelling.

Then Jonathan gave free play to his wild rage. "Murderer of your wife?" he said scornfully. "Fool! if it had been only the drops you gave her, she would be alive now; but nothing could have saved her. In the hurry of that night, Thomas, being just roused from sleep, gave you the other man's medicine, and handed yours to him. What you had was only good for infants; and Sister Julie might have drunk the whole bottleful without injury."

Mauer's gaze wandered uncertainly towards the speaker; a shudder passed over his dying form, and his brain made a powerful effort to penetrate the mists gathering over it.

"I did not kill Julie, and you knew it and never told me?" he stammered, with fast-failing voice.

"Certainly I knew it; but did you ever ask me about it? The other man had more forethought than you, and read the label before administering the dose to his child; and when he saw the name, he brought it back at once. It was two hours before he could get to my house again, and then Thomas had to prepare fresh medicine. Then I took the opium-drops intended for Sister Julie, and jumped on my horse; for although I knew she never could recover, I wanted to fulfil my duty as a physician, and do all I could to correct my servant's mistake. But I found her already dead; yes, from all appearances she must have been dead several hours. When I asked how that could have resulted from the drops, and saw your disturbed countenance, and how you became pale and faint, I thought you must have meditated the death of your wife, and with such design had given her a double dose which you intended should be fatal. I put the vial in my pocket, so that my servant's blunder might not be brought up against him or me. But Mauer," cried Jonathan, in a voice of frenzy, "when I stood by Don Manuel's death-bed and discovered your guilty love for Inez, while your wife stood in your way, everything became clear to me."

"You knew, Brother Jonathan, that I was bearing all the tortures of remorse, and yet gave me no word of explanation?" whispered the unhappy victim.

"That is not surprising. Do you know what hate is? You knew that I loved Inez. Can you imagine how I must have hated you who robbed me of her?" continued Jonathan, pitilessly.

"Yes, I knew you looked on yourself as a murderer! It answered my purpose not to have you think otherwise. It was sweet to me to see how this thought tortured you; it was a great satisfaction to know I held you in my power, like a butterfly on a needle, which it cannot get away from, and yet which remains quiescent and kills it painfully and slowly. Do you think I would not have brought you to justice if it had been true? Surely I would not have failed to do it; but Thomas, who knew all the circumstances and was with me in the mission, is here; he would have witnessed against me, had I accused you before the public. But I knew how to revenge myself on you for having stolen Inez from me, and for refusing me Carmen's hand. Your life must pay for Inez; your death will rob Carmen, as you have willed away your fortune from her for your supposed crime and left it to our community. Thus you will die at last, filled with regret at having wasted a life in unnecessary penance, and your silent lips will now take the old, dark story into the grave. I, however, will always feel an inward sense of triumph and delight that it was my foot which crushed you!"

He was silent, and stood with folded arms, looking down gloatingly on Mauer. He did not observe that in the shadow between the wall and the bed a head was raised. Suddenly a dark form rose, shadowy and indistinct. Jonathan grew pale. "Inez!" he gasped, and shrank back.

"No. Carmen; who has heard your cruel words, so that the silent lips shall not take the dark story of your wickedness to the grave. Wretch! devil incarnate! Can the earth hold such infamous scum? and has Heaven no lightning with which to strike you dead? Oh, father, my poor, persecuted father! There are no words to tell what you have suffered through this man!" And she threw herself again by the bed, and cast her arms about her dying parent.

But a glorious light of heavenly peace had settled on those pale features. With newly-acquired strength, he returned his daughter's embrace, raised his hands, and cried with accents of joy: "Child, rejoice, praise the Lord with me, for your father can now appear before his Judge, innocent of this crime. Blessed be God forever - amen!"

He stretched out his arms and sank back; one more sigh, as if the liberated soul were unfolding its wings to be borne on the breeze to heaven, and he lay still and peaceful in his daughter's arms.

With heart-rending sobs, she rained kisses on his hands, his lips, his brow; then closing his weary eyes, she whispered tenderly, amid scalding tears, "Dear father, sleep sweetly; you have earned it well!"

Some movement in the chamber of death attracted Carmen's notice, despite her overwhelming sorrow. She started up quickly. Who dared to intrude upon her thus? It was Jonathan, who was trying to make his escape from the room.

"Jonathan Fricke!" she cried, drawing herself up to her full height and at her call he seemed as if rooted to the ground. She passed around the bed, stepped to the table, and moved the lamp so as to throw a brighter light over the calm, placid features of the dead, around whose mouth a happy smile still lingered.

"Look on that face!" she said in a voice of command. Her face was all ablaze with righteous indignation, and she stood menacingly, but wondrously beautiful, before him, like an avenging angel ready to plunge the criminal down into the depths of hell.

"Do you see this holy, peaceful rest? Will you be able, some day, to lie down thus when the Lord demands an account of your life? You turn away your eyes, but you will never succeed in banishing the image of this face from your memory; it will haunt you wherever you go, by day and by night; its perpetual presence will be my father's revenge here below, and his accusation above, before the throne of judgment."

Humiliated and cowed, Jonathan stood motionless before

the scathing contempt of this noble woman.

"Do not think my father concealed his fault from me," she continued, her voice growing deeper and more threatening, as if the indignation surging up within her had lent it new power. "I know everything. I know how it happened; that, in a moment of weakness and temptation, the evil spirit drew near and enticed him. But he sinned in thought only; the All-merciful prevented the deed. How does his sin compare with yours, in the eyes of the One above?"

"I beseech you," began Jonathan in a cringing tone, "do not expose me to the community."

"Go!" she replied. "I will cast no slur on my father's memory by accusing you. Vengeance belongs to God alone."

She began to feel her strength giving way. The terrible agitation of her soul had exhausted her powers. At that moment she looked towards the open door which led to the next room, and saw Alexander and Agatha. She put her hands out to her husband as if seeking support and comfort and as he hastened towards her, she sank half-fainting on his breast.

"Carmen, my darling, my precious wife, this is a heavy sorrow which you have borne so long!" he said gently.

Agatha approached the bed and laid a linen cloth over the face of the one who had found rest at last.

"Carmen," she said, "your accusation is not needed. I will witness before the elders against this man, that he may no longer remain among us with his hypocritical piety and humility."

Jonathan looked at her bewildered.

"Is hell let loose?" he exclaimed, stamping his foot with rage. "Have you all conspired to destroy me?"

"Disturb not the dead with your unseemly words!" commanded Agatha. "To him mercy will be shown; but you, Jonathan, will be condemned here and in the world to come. Go!" She pointed to the door. He attempted to answer, but she cut his words short and repeated her command, "Go!"

After a moment's hesitation he disappeared out into the darkness.

Shortly after this dreadful scene, the sound of the trumpets announced to the people that Brother Mauer was dead; and soon it was noised abroad that Brother Jonathan had committed a great crime against the deceased, and the council of elders were seeking for him, to bring him to justice and punishment. Great excitement followed among these quiet Moravians, but Brother Jonathan was nowhere to be found. His disappearance was considered a proof of his guilt, and wherever the Brothers were stationed, in all parts of the world, notice was sent to them of Jonathan's crime, so that he would not be able to impose himself upon them, anywhere, as a Brother. He was publicly expelled from the faith, and it was decided by the council that the money left by the departed to his brethren, as an atonement for his sin, should be transferred to his daughter; but the Trautenaus preferred to let it go where the will had provided it should.

* * * * * *

With the first snow which fell about this time, a long and severe winter set in, which held the world bound for several months in ice and snow. But at last the mild south wind blew with its life-giving breath, and melted the icy mantle which had enveloped all things.

The thawed waters of the alder-pond then gave up from its depths a disfigured corpse, which had been concealed beneath its frozen surface during the severe season. It was the body of Brother Jonathan Fricke. The worthy laborer who chanced to find it was impressed with the idea that Jonathan had sought for salvation in its waters.

Had the guilt-laden man lost his way in the fogs of winter, and met his death by accident, or was he driven thither by a torturing conscience?

Choose from Thousands of 1stWorldLibrary Classics By

Adolphus WilliamWard
Aesop
Agatha Christie
Alexander Aaronsohn
Alexander Kielland
Alexandre Dumas
Alfred Gatty
Alfred Ollivant
Alice Duer Miller
Alice Turner Curtis
Alice Dunbar
Ambrose Bierce
Amelia E. Barr
Andrew Lang
Andrew McFarland Davis
Anna Sewell
Annie Besant
Annie Hamilton Donnell
Annie Payson Call
Anton Chekhov
Arnold Bennett
Arthur Conan Doyle
Arthur Ransome
Atticus
B. M. Bower
Basil King
Bayard Taylor
Ben Macomber
Booth Tarkington
Bram Stoker
C. Collodi
C. E. Orr
C. M. Ingleby
Carolyn Wells
Catherine Parr Traill
Charles A. Eastman
Charles Dickens
Charles Dudley Warner
Charles Farrar Browne
Charles Ives
Charles Kingsley
Charles Lathrop Pack
Charles Whibley
Charles Willing Beale
Charlotte M. Braeme
Charlotte M.Yonge
Clair W. Hayes
Clarence Day Jr.
Clarence E. Mulford

Clemence Housman
Confucius
Cornelis DeWitt Wilcox
Cyril Burleigh
D. H. Lawrence
Daniel Defoe
David Garnett
Don Carlos Janes
Donald Keyhole
Dorothy Kilner
Dougan Clark
E. Nesbit
E.P.Roe
E. Phillips Oppenheim
Edgar Allan Poe
Edgar Rice Burroughs
Edith Wharton
Edward J. O'Biren
John Cournos
Edwin L. Arnold
Eleanor Atkins
Elizabeth Cleghorn
Gaskell
Elizabeth Von Arnim
Ellem Key
Emily Dickinson
Erasmus W. Jones
Ernie Howard Pie
Ethel Turner
Ethel Watts Mumford
Eugenie Foa
Eugene Wood
Evelyn Everett-Green
Everard Cotes
F. J. Cross
Federick Austin Ogg
Ferdinand Ossendowski
Francis Bacon
Francis Darwin
Frances Hodgson Burnett
Frank Gee Patchin
Frank Harris
Frank Jewett Mather
Frank L. Packard
Frederick Trevor Hill
Frederick Winslow Taylor
Friedrich Kerst
Friedrich Nietzsche
Fyodor Dostoyevsky

Gabrielle E. Jackson
Garrett P. Serviss
Gaston Leroux
George Ade
Geroge Bernard Shaw
George Ebers
George Eliot
George MacDonald
George Orwell
George Tucker
George W. Cable
George Wharton James
Gertrude Atherton
Grace E. King
Grant Allen
Guillermo A. Sherwell
Gulielma Zollinger
Gustav Flaubert
H. A. Cody
H. B. Irving
H. G. Wells
H. H. Munro
H. Irving Hancock
H. Rider Haggard
H. W. C. Davis
Hamilton Wright Mabie
Hans Christian Andersen
Harold Avery
Harold McGrath
Harriet Beecher Stowe
Harry Houidini
Helent Hunt Jackson
Helen Nicolay
Hendy David Thoreau
Henrik Ibsen
Henry Adams
Henry Ford
Henry Frost
Henry James
Henry Jones Ford
Henry Seton Merriman
Henry Wadsworth
Longfellow
Henry W Longfellow
Herbert A. Giles
Herbert N. Casson
Herman Hesse
Homer
Honore De Balzac

M. CORVUS

Horace Walpole
Horatio Alger, Jr.
Howard Pyle
Howard R. Garis
Hugh Lofting
Hugh Walpole
Humphry Ward
Ian Maclaren
Israel Abrahams
J.G.Austin
J. Henri Fabre
J. M. Barrie
J. Macdonald Oxley
J. S. Knowles
J. Storer Clouston
Jack London
Jacob Abbott
James Allen
James Lane Allen
James Andrews
James Baldwin
James DeMille
James Joyce
James Oliver Curwood
James Oppenheim
James Otis
Jane Austen
Jens Peter Jacobsen
Jerome K. Jerome
John Burroughs
John F. Kennedy
John Gay
John Glasworthy
John Habberton
John Joy Bell
John Milton
John Philip Sousa
Jonathan Swift
Joseph Carey
Joseph Conrad
Joseph Jacobs
Julian Hawthrone
Julies Vernes
Justin Huntly McCarthy
Kakuzo Okakura
Kenneth Grahame
Kate Langley Bosher
L. A. Abbot
L. T. Meade
L. Frank Baum
Laura Lee Hope

Laurence Housman
Leo Tolstoy
Leonid Andreyev
Lewis Carroll
Lilian Bell
Lloyd Osbourne
Louis Tracy
Louisa May Alcott
Lucy Fitch Perkins
Lucy Maud Montgomery
Lydia Miller Middleton
Lyndon Orr
M. H. Adams
Margaret E. Sangster
Margaret Vandercook
Maria Edgeworth
Maria Thompson Daviess
Mariano Azuela
Marion Polk Angellotti
Mark Overton
Mark Twain
Mary Austin
Mary Cole
Mary Rowlandson
Mary Wollstonecraft
Shelley
Max Beerbohm
Myra Kelly
Nathaniel Hawthrone
O. F. Walton
Oscar Wilde
Owen Johnson
P.G.Wodehouse
Paul and Mable Thorn
Paul G. Tomlinson
Paul Severing
Peter B. Kyne
Plato
R. Derby Holmes
R. L. Stevenson
Rabindranath Tagore
Rahul Alvares
Ralph Waldo Emmerson
Rene Descartes
Rex E. Beach
Richard Harding Davis
Richard Jefferies
Robert Barr
Robert Frost
Robert Gordon Anderson
Robert L. Drake

Robert Lansing
Robert Michael Ballantyne
Robert W. Chambers
Rosa Nouchette Carey
Ross Kay
Rudyard Kipling
Samuel B. Allison
Samuel Hopkins Adams
Sarah Bernhardt
Selma Lagerlof
Sherwood Anderson
Sigmund Freud
Standish O'Grady
Stanley Weyman
Stella Benson
Stephen Crane
Stewart Edward White
Stijn Streuvels
Swami Abhedananda
Swami Parmananda
T. S. Ackland
The Princess Der Ling
Thomas A. Janvier
Thomas A Kempis
Thomas Anderton
Thomas Bailey Aldrich
Thomas Bulfinch
Thomas De Quincey
Thomas H. Huxley
Thomas Hardy
Thomas More
Thornton W. Burgess
U. S. Grant
Valentine Williams
Victor Appleton
Virginia Woolf
Walter Scott
Washington Irving
Wilbur Lawton
Wilkie Collins
Willa Cather
Willard F. Baker
William Makepeace
Thackeray
William W. Walter
Winston Churchill
Yei Theodora Ozaki
Young E. Allison
Zane Grey